More Praise for

"[Kevin Barry] isn't sparing with hi[...] [...]away lines are keepers. . . . What makes this b[...] [...]uch a satisfying read is that his memorable sentence-writing is in the service of well-constructed, moving stories." —*The New York Times*

"Stealthy and shimmering. . . . Darkness abounds in these 13 stories, though it takes its different forms: vileness, foreboding, ignorance, isolation, self-delusion, despair. . . . Often playful, comic, even gently so." —*The Boston Globe*

"Kevin Barry's best short stories are like a spade to the face. . . . There is a vividness to his writing that plants you immediately at its heart. . . . Phrases of sudden lyricism or savagery explode unexpectedly from banks of more conversational prose. . . . [Barry] earns comparison with the great and shamefully neglected VS Pritchett, whose short stories also employed pronounced comic means for serious, compassionate ends." —*The Guardian* (London)

"This collection is subtler, more poetic and more disturbing [than *City of Bohane*]. It reveals the menace of everyday life. . . . By the end of a story, Barry has me in full sympathy with someone I might edge away from on the train. His regard for characters big and small and capacity to be funny without playing them for cheap laughs recalls George Saunders." —*The New York Times Book Review*

"A pacy collection of thirteen modern tales about sozzled Irish men, neatly captured middle-class couples, sinisterly plotting old women and damaged lesbian hipsters. It's sharply observed, frequently rude, often very funny." —*The Independent on Sunday* (London)

"If these tales are built around marginalized figures, there's nothing uniform about Barry's storytelling voice. He does humor. He does high drama. He even dabbles in horror (of a kind). And he can handle just about any other narrative form you might think of. . . . If *City of Bohane* earned Barry a modicum of global literary stardom . . . this collection leaves no doubt that he's earned all that's come his way. Deeply humane and immensely funny, *Dark Lies the Island* is another testament to his many talents."   —*Star Tribune* (Minneapolis)

"From love, loss, regret and desire, [Kevin Barry] combines the real, the bizarre, and the mundane. His fluid style escorts the reader through a world that is funny, tragic, relentless, endearing. . . . A startlingly unique voice."   —*The Observer* (London)

"At the risk of indulging in cultural stereotypes, Barry is Irish: when he writes a story, he tells a story, and he's not afraid of a sentimental ending, if one presents itself. Along the way, he takes . . . contagious pleasure in his flawed, incorrigible people."   —Lorin Stein, *The Paris Review*

"[Kevin Barry's] prose is almost literally indescribable. . . . It's not hard to see a devoted following accrue around this singular talent."
                                                          —*Irish Independent*

"[*Dark Lies the Island*] shares the virtues that made *Bohane* such an astonishment—prose that rollicks and judders and constantly delights; a keen ear for the spoken language of Barry's native western Ireland; and above all . . . a way of lassoing moments of mystery that have the power to transform the lives of Barry's characters, a motley Irish medley of disturbed young women, devious old spinsters, blocked poets, thugs, boozers, exiles, and tortured civil servants. There is rich music, high humor, and deep blackness on every page. . . . You must read this impossibly gifted, unspeakably lovely Irish writer."   —*The Millions*

"A wonderful book packed with glinting comedic observations, sentences that run through you like electric shocks, and characters it's tough to get enough of."   —*Guernica*, Favorite Books from 2013

"[Kevin Barry] has a singular voice and imagination. . . . Satire is something that Barry excels at as he zeroes in on the hilarity and the dangers—especially the dangers—of small-town Irish ennui and insularity. . . . *Dark Lies the Island* achieves what any good story collection strives to, displaying Barry's vast range of talent and writerly moods."
—*Irish America*

"The writing is spectacular, alternately stately and hurried, occasionally clipped but never languid, steeped in the vernacular but never lacking precision, and very often pulsing with the rhythm of iambic pentameter. Smashing, compulsively readable stuff: Barry will be a household name, and soon." —*Booklist*, starred review

"Barry offers a second story collection that offers all the best qualities of his IMPAC award-winning debut novel, *City of Bohane*—the dark humor, apt characterization, and sharply condensed emotion, so well contained by the beautiful sentences." —*Library Journal*, starred review

"Irish lyricism shines throughout the collection. . . . Barry writes stories that are character-driven, archetypical yet magnetic, pushing toward realism's edge where genre becomes irrelevant." —*Kirkus Reviews*

"There are a lot of pleasures to be had. . . . There's his way with language—a bent form of Irish that makes the most mundane language, like those of the mileage-obsessed locals at the hotel bar in 'Fjord of Killary,' somehow hilarious. Then there's the pleasure of safely spending time in the company of people you might well cross the street to avoid." —*Publishers Weekly*, starred review

DARK LIES
THE ISLAND

DARK LIES THE ISLAND

Stories by
Kevin Barry

Graywolf Press

First published by Jonathan Cape, The Random House Group Ltd, London

Portions of this work have appeared in the following:
'Fjord of Killary' appeared in the *New Yorker.*
'Beer Trip to Llandudno' appeared in *New Irish Short Stories* (Faber & Faber)
    and *Tin House.*
'Ernestine and Kit' appeared in *Columbia.*
'Doctor Sot' appeared in *Best European Fiction 2011* (Dalkey Archive).
'The Girls and the Dogs' appeared in *Sharp Sticks, Driven Nails* (Stinging Fly Press).
'White Hitachi' appeared in the *John McGahen Yearbook,* vol 2 (National University
    of Ireland, Galway).

This publication is made possible, in part, by the voters of Minnesota through a
Minnesota State Arts Board Operating Support grant, thanks to a legislative appro-
priation from the arts and cultural heritage fund, and through a grant from the Wells
Fargo Foundation Minnesota. Significant support has also been provided by Target, the
McKnight Foundation, Amazon.com, and other generous contributions from founda-
tions, corporations, and individuals. To these organizations and individuals we offer our
heartfelt thanks.

Published by Graywolf Press
250 Third Avenue North, Suite 600
Minneapolis, Minnesota 55401

www.graywolfpress.org

Published in the United States of America

ISBN 978-1-55597-651-4 (cloth)
ISBN 978-1-55597-688-0 (paper)

2 4 6 8 9 7 5 3 1
First Graywolf Paperback, 2015

Library of Congress Control Number: 2014950987

Cover design: The Random House Group Ltd

CONTENTS

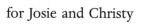

for Josie and Christy

ACROSS THE ROOFTOPS

Early one summer morning, I sat with her among the rooftops of the city and the fat white clouds moved slowly above
us – it was so early as to be a city lost in sleep, and she was
really very near to me. My want for her was intense and
long-standing – three months, at least; an eternity – and I
was close enough to see the opaque down of her bare arms,
each strand curling like a comma at its tip, and the tiny
scratched flecks of dark against the hazel of her eyes. She
was just a stretch and a clasp away. The city beneath was
lost to the peaceful empty moments of 5 a.m. – it might
be a perfect Saturday of July. All I had to do was make the
move.

Nor was it my imagination that her shoulder inclined
just slightly towards me, that there was a dip in the way
she held it, the shoulder bare also beneath the strap of
her vest top. The shoulder's dip must signal an opening.

'Now I don't want to sound painfully cool here?' I said.

'I believe you,' she said.

'But you may be looking at the man who introduced
Detroit techno to the savages of Cork city.'

We talked about the music and the clothes and the pills
and the hours we had spent together – the nightclub, and
then the party at the flat that was rented by friends, all of

1

whom were panned out inside now, asleep or halfways there, and we had climbed onto the rooftop to smoke a joint and see the day come through. Every line had the dry inflected drag of irony – feeling was unmentionable. We talked about everything except the space between us.

I sat on my hands.

I thought about maybe kissing her shoulder. How would that be for a move? It would be the work of two seconds – a lean-to, a planting of the lips, a withdrawal. And a shy little glance to follow.

'I should maybe think about going,' she said.

I really needed to make the move.

'Don't yet,' I said.

The pool of silence that was the city beneath us was broken but infrequently – a scratch of car noise from a cab rank, the tiny bark of a dog from high in the estates somewhere, very distant, the sound of the traffic lights turning on the corner of Washington Street and Grand Parade. Across the way the church and its steeple, the grey of old devotion, the greened brass of its dome.

I turned towards her and I looked at her directly and her eyes braved me to make the move.

'So any plans for Saturday?' I said.

I read again the disappointment in her – she was urging me on but onwards I could not make ground.

'Depends,' she said.

Her shoulder dipped a fraction again. Now was the moment. I sat on my hands and looked out across the rooftops and saw nothing, registered nothing but the hard quickening beat of my heart.

'So . . . how's it you know Cecille again?' I said.

She sighed and explained the connection – it was through the university, they had shared a place on French's Quay as first years.

'And-how-do-you-know-Cecille?'

She said it in an exaggeratedly bored tone – an automated drone, the words running into each other; a mockery.

The flat high on Washington Street was Cecille's – Cecille had in her bedroom loudly been fucking some boy for most of the night; Cecille had no trouble ever making the moves.

'Cecille's had a good night anyway,' I said.

'Yeah,' she said.

Maybe I should just ask, I thought. Can I kiss you? How would that sound?

A gull descended to the lip of the church's roof. Across the breadth of the street, the mad stare of its eye was vivid and comical and a taunt to me.

I allowed my left hand to emerge from beneath my buttock and I let it travel the space between us, along the cool stone of the ledge, and I placed my fingers lightly on hers.

No response.

I listened for a change in her breathing but nothing. She was still even and steady and I turned to look at her and blithely still she looked out and across the rooftops. She did not incline her head towards me. And she did not speak at all.

I drew back my fingers but only by an inch or two.

I looked to see if she would withdraw her hand to a safer distance but she did not.

She breathed evenly.

Hard rasps of jungle panic ripped at my chest inside.

I thought – what's the worst that can happen here? The worst that can happen is I lurch and she recoils. So much worse not to try.

'So all I have to do now,' I said, 'is make the move.'

'Jesus Christ,' she said.

'What?'

'You're killing this stone dead,' she said.

But she did not get up from the ledge. She did not leave my side. She allowed the silence to swell and fill out again. Now birdsong taunted from the direction of Bishop Lucey Park. What if I left it to her to make the move? Procreation would end and the world would stop spinning.

The birdsong rose up now and strung its notes along the rooftops and linked them in a jagged line, the rise and fall of the steeples and chimneys was as though a musical notation. There was dead quiet from the flat inside. The last awake, we had the morning to ourselves.

'I really like you,' I said.

'Okay,' she said.

'I mean really really.'

So very hard to put the words out but they were on the air and at their work now. I turned to look at her and she turned but to look away. I saw that a flush had risen to her cheek. The perfect knit of her collarbone as it turned, and flawless brown from a good June the smooth curve of the shoulder. Like rounded stone made smooth by water. It was as if my words had just flown up into the white sky above and softly imploded there, as if an answer was not needed.

'Okay,' I said.

This meant everything. All of summer would be coloured by this. She did not seem to breathe then. I kept my eyes

4

fixed on her, as she looked anywhere but at me, and I counted the seconds away as she did not turn to face me.

In my evil dreams I had seen myself approach her with lascivious intent – with a cold thin cruel sexual mouth just parted slight-ways – and I went deep then to find a way to make this suave magic come real. Still, something in her presence unmanned me; perhaps it was the sense that I was aiming too high. She was really quite beautiful.

'Turn to me,' I said.

She laughed but it was only a tiny laugh and it had the trace of shock in it – I was forceful now out of nowhere.

And she turned to me.

I leaned in without pause – I did not allow the words to jumble up in my head and forbid me – and I placed my lips on hers.

She responded well enough – the opening of the lips was made, our jawbones worked slowly and devoutly, but . . . we did not ascend to the heavens; the kiss did not take.

After I don't know how long – maybe half a minute, maybe a little more – she placed very lightly on my chest the tips of her fingers and the tiny pressure she applied there told me it was over, already, the pressure was of a fuse that fed directly from her heart. Gently so with her fingertips she pushed me back to break the kiss.

She turned quickly to look away and I turned as quickly to look in the opposite direction. My heart opened and took in every black poison the morning could offer.

Midsummer. Slant of the sun coming through the white-clouded sky then, and the church across the way drew its own shade over half of Washington Street; a fat pigeon flew beneath the eave of the church and only the heavy beat of its wings on the air broke the dark spell that had formed about us. I turned to look at her, and she responded with a half-smile, half sorrowful. She placed her palms face down on the ledge and pushed herself to a stand. Languid, the movement, to let me know what I was missing.

'I'm going to go,' she said.

I nodded as coolly as I could. That I could muster even the tiniest measure of cool was credit to my resilience. I was resilient as the small medieval city beneath – throw a siege upon me and I will withstand it. She crawled through the Velux window to the flat inside, and I heard after a few moments the turn and click on the flat's door; then her footsteps on the stair. With her steps' fading, the summer went, even as the sun came higher across the rooftops and warmed the stone ledge and the slates, and I looked out across the still, quiet city, and I sat there for hours and for months and for years. I sat there until all that had been about us had faded again to nothing, until the sound of the crowd died and the music had ended, and we all trailed home along the sleeping streets, with youth packed away, and life about to begin.

WIFEY REDUX

This is the story of a happy marriage but before you throw up and turn the page let me say that it will end with my face pressed hard into the cold metal of the Volvo's bonnet, my hands cuffed behind my back, and my rights droned into my ear – this will occur in the car park of a big-box retail unit on the Naas Road in Dublin.

We were teenage sweethearts, Saoirse and I. She was exquisite, and seventeen; I was a couple of years the older. She was blonde and wispily slight with a delicate, bone-china complexion. Her green eyes were depthless pools – I'm sorry, but this is a love story – and I drowned in them. She had amazing tits, too, small but textbook, perfectly cuppable, and an outstanding arse. I mean literally an outstanding arse. Lasciviously draw in the air, while letting your tongue loll and eyes roll, the abrupt curve of a perfect, flab-free butt-cheek: she had a pair of those. It was shelved, the kind of arse my father used to say (in wry and manly side-mouthing) you could settle a mug of tea on. Also, she had a raunchy laugh and unwavering taste and she understood me. In retrospect, with the due modesty of middle age, I accept there wasn't that much to understand. I was a moderately poetical kid, and moderately rebellious, but diligent in my studies all the same, and three months out of college I had a comfortable nook secured in the civil service. We got married when Saoirse was twenty-one and I was twenty-three. That seems impossibly young now but this was the late 'eighties. And we made a picture – I was a gorgeous kid myself. A Matt Dillon-type, people used to say, which dates me. But your dates can work out, and we were historically lucky in the property market. We bought a fabulous old terrace house with a view to the seafront in Dun Laoghaire. We could lie in bed and watch the ships roll out across Dublin Bay, all lighted and melancholy in the night. We'd lie amid the flicker of candles and feast on each other. We couldn't believe our luck.

We had bought the place for a song. Some old dear had died in it, and it had granny odours, so it took a while to strip back the flock wallpaper and tan-coloured linoleum, but it was a perfect dream that we unpeeled. The high ceilings, the bay windows, the palm tree set in the front garden: haughty Edwardiana. We did it up with the sweat of our love and frequently broke off from our DIY tasks to fuck each other histrionically (it felt like we were running a race) on the stripped floorboards. The house rose 35 per cent in value the year after we bought it. It has since octupled in value.

Those early years of our marriage were perfect bliss. Together, we made a game out of life – everything was an adventure; even getting the tyres filled, even doing the groceries. We laughed a lot. We tiddled each other in the frozen foods aisle. We bit each other lustfully in the back row of the pictures at the late show, Saturdays. We made ironical play of our perfect marriage. She called me 'Hubby' and I called her 'Wifey'. I can see her under a single sheet, with her bare, brown legs showing, and coyly in the morning she calls to me as I dress:

'Hubby? Don't go just yet . . . Wifey needs . . . attendance.'

'Oh but Wifey, it's past eight already and . . .'

'What's the wush, Hubby?'

Saoirse could not (and cannot) pronounce the letter 'R' – a rabbit was a wabbit – which made her even more cute and bonkable.

I rose steadily in the civil service. I was pretty much unsackable, unless I whipped out a rifle in the canteen or raped somebody in the photocopier room. Hubby went to work, and Wifey stayed at home, but we were absolutely an equal partnership. Together, in slow-mo, we jogged the dewy, early-morning park. Our equity by the month swelled, the figures rolling ever upwards with gay abandon. The electricity of our enraptured smiles – ! ! – could have powered the National fucking Grid. Things just couldn't get any better, and they did.

In the third year of our marriage, a girl-child was born to us. Our darling we named Ellie, and she was a marvel. She was the living image of her beautiful mother, and I was doubly in love – I pushed her stroller along the breezy promenade, the Holyhead ferry hooted, and my heart soared with the black-backed gulls. Ellie slept eight hours a night from day one. Never so much as a teething pain. A perfect, placid child, and mantelpiece-pretty. We were so lucky I came to fear some unspeakable tragedy, some deft disintegration. But the seasons as they unrolled in south County Dublin were distinct and lovely, and each had its scheduled joys – the Easter eggs, the buckets and spades, the Halloween masks, the lovely tinsel schmaltz of Crimbo. Hubby, Wifey, Baby Ellie – heaven had come down and settled all about us.

If, over the subsequent years, the weight of devotion between Saoirse and I ever so fractionally diminished – and I mean *tinily* – this, too, I felt, was healthy. We probably needed to pull back, just a tad, from the obsessive quality of our love for each other. This minuscule diminishing was evident, perhaps, in the faint sardonic note that entered our conversation. Say when I came home from work in the evening, and she said:

'Well, *Hubby?*'

With that kind of dry up note at the end of a sentence, that sarcastic stress? And I would answer in kind:

'Well, *Wifey?*'

Of course the century turned, and early middle age slugged into the picture, and our arses dropped. Happens. And sure, I began to thicken a little around the waist. And yes, unavoidably, the impromptu fucking tends to die off a bit when you've a kid in the house. But we were happy still, just a little more calmly so, and I repeat that this is the story of a happy, happy marriage. (Pounds table twice for emphasis.)

Not that I didn't linger sometimes in memory. How could I not? I mean Saoirse, when she was seventeen, was . . . erotic perfection. I could never desire anyone more than I did Saoirse back then. It was painful, almost, that I had wanted her so badly, and it had felt sinful, almost (I was brought up Catholic), to be able to sate my lust for her, at will, whenever I wanted, in whatever manner I wanted, and for so many ecstatic years.

I'm not saying she hasn't aged well. She remains an extremely handsome woman. She has what my mother used to call an excellent hold of herself. Certainly, there is a little weight on her now, and that would have seemed unimaginable on those svelte, fawnish, teenage limbs, but as I have said, I'm no Twiggy myself these days. We like creamy pasta dishes flecked with lobster bits. We like ludicrously expensive chocolate. The kind with chilli bits baked in and a lavender dusting. And yes, occasionally, in the small hours, I suffer from . . . weeping jags. As the ships roll out remorselessly across Dublin Bay. And fine, let's get it all out there, let's – Saoirse has developed a Pinot Grigio habit that would knock a fucking horse.

But we are happy. We love each other. And we are dealing.

Because we married so young, however, and because we had our beautiful Ellie so early in life, we have that strange sensation of still being closely attuned to the operatics of the teenage world even now as our daughter has entered it. It's almost as if we never left it ourselves, and we know all the old steps of the dance still as Ellie pelts through that skittle sequence of drugs, music, fashion, melancholia, suicidal ideation and, well, sex.

The difficult central fact of this thing: Ellie is now seventeen years old and everything about her is a taunt to man. The hair, the colouring, the build. Her sidelong glance, and the hoarseness of her laugh, and the particular way she pokes the tip of her tongue from the corner of her mouth in sardonic dismissal, and the hammy, poppy-eyed stare that translates as:

'Are you for *weal?*'

No, she can't say her Rs either. And she wears half-nothing. Hot pants, ripped tights, belly tops, and she has piercings all over. A slash of crimson lippy. Thigh-high boots.

Now understand that this is not about to get weird and fucked up but I need to point out that she is identical to Saoirse at that age. I am just being brutally honest here. And I would plead that the situation is not unusual. It's just one of those things you're supposed to keep shtum about. Horribly often, our beautiful, perfect daughters emerge into a perfect facsimile of how our beautiful, desirable wives had been, back then, when they were young. And slim. And sober. There is a horrid poignancy to it. And to even put this stuff down on paper looks wrong. There are certain people (hello, Dr Murtagh!) who would see this and think: your man is bad again. So I should just get to the story of how the trouble started. And, of course, it concerns my hatred for the boys who flock around my beautiful daughter.

Oh, trust me. Every hank of hair and hormones with the price of a lip ring in the borough of Dun Laoghaire has been panting after our Ellie. But she flicked them all away, one after the other, nothing lasted for more than an innocent date or two. Not until young and burly Aodhan McAdam showed up on the scene.

Even saying the horrible, smug, hiccupy syllables of that fucker's name makes me retch. He wasn't her usual type, so immediately I was worried. The usual type – so far as it had been established – was black-clad, pale-skinned, basically depressed-looking, given to eyeliner and guitar cases, Columbine types, sniper material, little runts in duster coats, addicted to their antihistamine inhalers, self-harmers, yadda-yadda, but basically innocent. I knew by the way she carried herself that she did not succumb to them. A father can tell – although this is another of the facts you're supposed to keep shtum about. But then – hear the brush and rattle of doom's timpani drums – enter Aodhan McAdam.

'Howya doin' boss-man?'

This, quickly, became his ritual greeting when I answered the door, evenings, and found him in his track pants and Abercrombie & Fitch polo shirt on the chequered tiles of our porch. He typically accompanied the greeting with a pally little punch on my upper arm and a big, toothy grin. He was seventeen, six two, with blonde, floppy hair, and about eight million quids' worth of dental work. Looked like he'd been raised on prime beef and full-fat milk. Handsome as a movie star and so easy in his skin. One of those horrible, mid-Atlantic twangs – these kids don't even sound fucking Irish any more – and broad as a jeep; I had no doubt he could beat the shit out of me. Which meant that I would have to surprise him.

I knew after the first two weeks that they were fucking. It was the way she carried herself – she was little-girl no more. And what did her mother do about this? She went and fetched another bottle of Pinot Grigio from the fridge.

'Saoirse, we need to talk about what's going on back there?'

Wrong, I know, you're supposed to leave these things be. But I couldn't . . . I couldn't *not* bring it up. It was poisoning me.

Saoirse and I were in the front den. We keep the bigger TV in there, and the coffee table we commissioned from the Artisans-with-Aids programme, and a retro 'fifties couch in a burnt-orange shade that our shapes have settled into – unpleasantly, it makes it look like we have arses the size of boulders – and stacks upon stacks of DVDs climb the walls, just about every box set yet issued.

'I suppose you know,' I said, 'that they're, well . . . you know.'

'Don't,' Saiorse said.

I sighed and left the den. The way it worked, Ellie had the use of the sitting room down back of the ground floor; no teenager wants to sit with her parents. She'd had a decorater in – it was got up in like a purple-and-black scheme – and she had a really fabulous Eames couch we'd got at auction for her sixteenth, and I went down there to check on Aodhan and herself. The shade was down, and they were watching some hip-hop crap on satellite, and they were under a duvet. This was a summer evening.

'Yo, Popiscle,' Ellie said.

'Hey,' Aodhan McAdam said, and leered at me.

I unleashed the coldest look I could summon and tried to say something and felt like I had a mouthful of marbles. I went back to the front den. I settled into the massive arse shape on my side of the couch.

'Do you realise,' I said, 'that they're under a duvet back there?'

'Mmm-hmm?'

Saoirse was watching a *Wire* episode with crew commentary and was nose deep in a bucket-sized glass of Pinot Grigio. She drank it ice-cold – I could see the splinters of frozen crystals in there.

'I mean what the fuck are they doing under a duvet? It's July!'

She turned to me, and smiled benignly.

'I think we can pwesume,' she said, 'that she's jackin' him off.'

'Lovely,' I said.

14

'Ellie's seventeen,' she said. 'The fuck do you think she's doing?'

'That *fucking* little McAdam bastard . . .'

'Not so little,' Saoirse said. 'And actually he's kinda hot?'

You're supposed to just deal. But my brain would not stop whirring. I lay there that night in bed, and I was under siege. Random images came at me which I will not describe. I was nauseous. I knew it was a natural thing. I knew there was no stopping it. And as the morning surfaced on the bay, I tried to accept it. But I got out of the bed and I felt like I'd fought a war. I thought, maybe it's better that he's a rugby type rather than one of the sniper types. At least maybe he's healthier.

That evening, after work, as I took my walk along the prom, with the cold sea oblivious, I saw them: the rugby boys. They hang out by a particular strip of green down there, sitting around the rain shelter, or tossing a ball about, and chortling all the time, chortling, with their big shiteater grins and testosterone. They all have the floppy hair, the polo shirts in soft pastels, the Canterbury track pants, the mid-Atlantic twangs. Aodhan McAdam was among them, and he saw me, and grinned, and he made a pair of pistols with his fingers and fired them at me.

Ka-pow, he mouthed.

Ha-ha, I grinned back.

He was no doubt giving the rest of the scrum a full account about what went on beneath the duvet. Of course he was! And later he was back for more. Bell rings about ten: orthodontic beam on porch. In fact, he appeared to have pretty much moved into the house. Every night now he was among us.

15

'Babes!' she squealed, and she raced down the hallway, and leapt onto him, and right there – right in front of me! – he cupped her butt-cheek.

Now often, between box-set episodes, Saoirse and I hang in the kitchen – it's maybe our fave space, and it's tricked out with as much cutesy, old-timey shit as a soul could reasonably stomach. The Aga. The stoneware pots from Puglia. The St Brigid's Cross made out of actual, west of Ireland reeds for an ethnic-type touch. We snack hard and we just, like, sway with the kitchen vibe? But now Ellie and Aodhan were invading. Eighteen times a night they were out of the back room and attacking the fridge. Saoirse just smiled, fondly, as they ploughed into the hummus, the olives, the flatbreads, the cold cuts, the blue cheese, the Ben 'n' Jerry's, the lavender-dusted chocolate from Fallon & Byrne. I watched the motherfucker from the island counter – the way he wolfed the stuff down was unreal.

'Do they feed you at your own place at all, Aodhan?' I said, wryly.

He chortled, and he took out a six pack of Petit Filous yoghurts, and he made for the couch-and-duvet in my back room. He mock-punched me in the gut as he passed by.

'This ol' boy's runnin' on heavy fuel,' he said, and he mussed my hair, or what's left of it.

Later, in the den, I turned to Saoirse:

'He's treating me like a bitch,' I said.

She was freezeframing bits of *The Wire* that featured the gay killer Omar because she had a thing for him. She had lately been waking in the night and crying out his name.

'So what are you going to do about it?' she said.

'I know they're fucking,' I said. 'I can just . . . smell it?'

16

'You need to talk to Doctor Murtagh about this,' she said.

'Meaning?'

'Meaning cognitive fucking thewapy,' she said. 'Meaning medication time. Meaning this is looking like a bweakdown-type thing again?'

All over the house, I felt like I could hear him . . . chomping? You know sometimes, in a plane, when your ears are weird, and they flip out the food trays, and you chew, and you can hear the jaw motions of your own mastication in a loud, amped, massively unpleasant way? It was like I was hearing that all over the house –

Aodhan!

Chomping!

Also, he was using the downstairs loo, under the stairs, and of course he pissed like a prize stallion. Saoirse thought it was all marvellous, and she talked increasingly about how hot she thought he was, as hot almost as Omar. We're talking a lunk but angelically pretty – like a beefy choirboy that could mangle a bear? Fucking hideous.

Then summer thickened and there was a heatwave. We garden, and we have a terrific deck – done out with all this Tunisian shit we bought off the lepers in Zarzis – over-looking the back lawn. During the heatwave, Aodhan and Ellie took over the deck space. I watched from the kitchen – I was deveining some king prawns while Saoirse expertly pestled a coriander-seed-and-lime-zest marinade. Ellie lay face down on the lounger, in a string bikini, and he sat on the lounger's edge, and with his big sausagey fingers he untied the top of the bikini, and pushed the straps gently back. Then he shook the lotion bottle, rubbed a squirt of it onto his palms, and began to massage it in, super-slow, like some fucking porno set-up. Through the open window I heard her throaty little moans, and I saw the way she turned to him, adoringly, and he bent down and whispered to her, and she squealed.

'Next thing,' I said to Saoirse, 'they're actually going to have it off in front of us.'

'What is she, a nun?'

'I've had enough of this,' I said.

I flung the prawns into the Belfast sink and I stormed out of the house. I bought cigarettes for the first time in six months and lit one right there on the forecourt of the Topaz. I smoked, and I took off along the prom. I passed the rugby boys' rain shelter, and it was deserted, and I saw that there was an amount of graffiti scrawled around the back wall of the shelter. I went to have a closer look.

Nicknames, stuff about schools-rugby rivals, so-and-so loves such-and-such, or so-and-so loves ???, but then, prominently, this:

ELLIE P THE BLO-JOB QUEEN

B-L-O! And P! That they had used my surname's initial for emphasis, the P of my dead father's Prendergast! I went and power-walked the length of the pier and back three times. A glorious summer evening, and busy on the pier, with friends and neighbours all about – but I just ignored them all; I pelted up and down, with my arms swinging, and I ground my teeth, and I cried a little (a lot), and I smoked the pack.

I could see the neighbours thinking:

Is he not great again?

Later, in the den:

Aodhan had gone home, and I could hear the *thunk, shlank, whumpf* of her music from upstairs, and Saoirse had gone into her keeping-an-eye-on-me mode; she was all concerned and hand-holdy now.

'I think we can pwesume, hon,' she said, 'that he didn't, like, white it himself?'

'A gentleman!' I said. 'But even so he's been mouthing off, hasn't he? And it doesn't bother you at all that she's . . .'

I couldn't finish it.

'She's seventeen, Jonathan.'

'I say we front her.'

'This is nuts. And say what? That she shouldn't be giving blow jobs?'

'Please, Saoirse . . .'

'I was giving blow jobs at seventeen.'

'Congratulations.'

'As you well know.'

'But I wasn't mouthing off about it, was I? I was keeping it to myself!'

'Just leave it, Jonathan . . .'

Again that night I hardly slept. I developed this incessant buzzing sound in my head. It sounded like I had a broken strip light in there. More images came at me, and you can picture exactly what they were:

Ellie, descending.

And big Aodhan McAdam – ! – grinning.

The next morning I went to her room. Fuck it, I was going to be strong. There was going to be a conversation about Respect. For herself, for her home, for her parents. For duvets. I knocked, crisply, twice, and I pushed in the

19

door, and I could feel that my forehead was taut with self-righteousness (or whatever), and I found her in a sobbing mess on the bed.

Suicidal!

Ellie's tears nuke my innards.

'Oh, babycakes!' I wailed 'What is it!'

I threw myself on the bed. So much for the Respect conversation. Aodhan, it turned out, had taken his oral gratification and skedaddled. It was so over.

She was inconsolable. We had the worst Saturday morning of all time in our house. Which is saying a great deal. She was between rage and tears and when she is upset she behaves appallingly, my angel. It started right off, at breakfast:

A sunny Saturday, heaven-sent, in peejays – it should have been perfection. Saoirse was sitting at the island counter, trembling, as she ate pinhead porridge with acai fruit and counted off the hours till she could start glugging back the ice-cold Pinot Grigio. I was scraping an anti-death spread the colour of Van Gogh's sunflowers onto a piece of nine-grain artisanal toast. Ellie was vexing between flushes of crimson rage and sobbing fits and making a sound like a lung-diseased porpoise.

'Oh please, Ell?' I said. 'It's only been, like . . .'

'Eleven weeks!' she cried. 'Eleven weeks of my fucking life I gave that dickwad!'

'Look, baby, I know it doesn't seem like it now? But you'll get over this and it might work out for the best and . . .'

And maybe the blow-job rep will start to fade, I didn't say.

'What's this?' she said.

20

She held a box of muesli in her hand.

'It's a box of muesli,' I said.

'No it is not,' she said.

Admittedly, it was an own-brand line from a mid-range supermarket – a rare anomaly.

'Ah, Ellie, it's fine, look, it's actually quite tasty . . .'

She turned the box upside down and emptied the muesli onto the limestone flags that had cost peasants their dignity to hump over from County Clare.

'This is not *actual* ceweal,' she said. 'This is, like, twibute ceweal?'

She began with her bare feet to slowly crush the muesli into the flagstones. Deliberately grinding up and down, with a steady rhythm to her step, like a French yokel mashing grapes, or a chick on a Stairmaster set to a high gradient.

'I want him back,' she said.

'Ah, look, Ellie, I mean . . .'

'I want Aodhan back.'

She came across the flags and caught me by the peejay lapels.

'And I want him back today!'

I fell to my knees and hugged her waist.

'But this is madness!' I cried.

Generally speaking, in the run of a life, when you find yourself using the expression –

'But this is madness!'

– you can take it that things are not going to quickly improve. It was half ten in the morning but Saoirse didn't give a toss any more and she went to the fridge and took the cork from a half-drunk bottle of Pinot Grigio. With her teeth.

So! The next development!

I was sent to have a heart-to-heart with Aodhan McAdam. He had, of course, switched his phone off – they are by seventeen experts in avoidance tactics. And Ellie could not and would not lower her dignity by going to find him herself. And Saoirse hadn't left the house in eleven months, except for Vida Pura™ blood transfusions, Dakota hot-stone treatments, and Beach Body Bootcamp (abandoned). So it was down to me. I was to find out his mood, his motives, his intentions. Essentially, I was to win him back. Saoirse was as intent on getting him back as Ellie. He was male youth, after all, and she liked having that stuff around the house.

It turned out that McAdam worked a Saturday job. Oh right, I thought, so he's going with the humble shit – a Saturday job! He worked at this DIY warehouse on the Naas Road. I got in the Volvo and rolled. I played a motivational CD. N'gutha Ba'al, the Zambian self-confidence guru, told me in his rich, honeyed timbre that I had a warrior's inner glow and the spirit of a cheetah. I cried a little (a lot) at this. I felt husky and brave and stout-hearted but the feeling was fleet as the light on the bay. Traffic was scant but scary. Cars edged out at the intersections in abrupt, skittery move-ments. Trucks loomed, and the sound of their exhausts was horrifyingly amplified. Pedestrians were straight out of a bad dream. Everybody's hair looked odd. I drove through the south side of the city, tightened my grip on the wheel and tried to remember to breathe in the belly. The Volvo was grinding like an assassin as I pulled into the Do-It-Rite! car park. I tried to play the thing like I was an ordinary Joe, a Saturday-man just out on an errand, but I knew at once

I wanted to climb up the store's signage and rip down that exclamation mark

!

from Do-It-Rite!

I stormed – stormed! – towards the entrance but that didn't work out, as the automatic doors did not register my presence as a human being. So I had to take a little step back and approach the doors again – but still they would not part – and I reversed three steps, four, and approached yet again, but still they would not part, and in my shame I raised my eyes to the heavens, and I saw that the letters of the Do-It-Rite! signage were so flimsily attached, with just brackets and screws, and this too was an outrage – the shoddiness of the fix. Then a Saturday-man approached and the doors glided open and I entered the store in the slipstream of his normalcy.

I hunted the aisles for Aodhan McAdam. They were shooting day-for-night in the vast warehouse space, it was luridly strip-lit, and I prowled by the paint racks, the guttering supplies, the mops and hinges, the masonry nails, the rat traps and the laminate flooring kits, and some cronky half-smothered yelps of rage escaped my throat as I walked, and every Saturday-man I passed did a double-take on me. The place was the size of a half-dozen soccer pitches patchworked together, and the staff wore yellow dungaree cover-alls, so that they could be picked out for DIY advice, and eventually I saw up top of a set of cover-alls the blond, floppy hair, the megawatt grin and the powerful jaw muscles, those hideous chompers.

'Aodhan!'

The grin turned to me, and it was so enormous it dazzled

his features to an indistinctness, I saw just that exclamation mark

!

from the Do-It-Ritc! – but when he focused, the grin died, at once, right there.

'Jonathan?'

I went to him, and I smiled, and I took gently his elbow in my hand.

'Can we talk, Aodhan?'

'Sure, man, I mean . . .'

Now it is a rare enough occurrence in contemporary life that the occasion presents itself for truly felt speech. We are trapped – all of us – behind this glaring wash of irony. But in the quietest aisle of the Do-It-Rite! that Saturday – drylining accessories – as Aodhan McAdam and I squatted discreetly on our haunches, I spoke honestly, and powerfully, and from the heart.

'Listen,' I said, 'I know about the blow jobs. That's perfectly natural. I was getting blow jobs myself when I was seventeen. I wasn't broadcasting the fact, and I could *spell*, but I was . . .'

He tried to rise from his haunches, he tried to get away, but I had this strange animal strength (your eyebrows ascend, Dr Murtagh), and I kept his bony elbow clamped in my claw, and I lasered my eyes into his, and he was scared enough, I could see that.

I said:

'Ellie Prendergast, or should I say *Ellie P*, is the most beautiful girl in this city. She is an absolute fucking angel. If you hurt her, I will kill you. I'm telling you this now so you can give yourself a chance.'

I slapped him once across the face. It was a manic shot with plenty of sting to it. I told him of youth's fleeting nature. I told him he didn't realise how quickly all this would pass. I told him how it had been for me. I spoke of the darknesses that can so quickly seep between the cracks of a life. I told him of the images I had witnessed and voices I had heard. He began to cry in fear. I told him how my Wifey had been plagued by evil faeries in the night – oh it was all coming out! – and how my Ellie was to me a deity to be worshipped, and I would protect her with my life.

'I have Type 1 diabetes!' he sobbed. 'I can't deal with this shit!'

Oh but I laid it on with a motherfucking trowel. I brought him to the pits of despair and showed him around. My threats were veiled and made stranger by the serenity of my smile. I said I expected him on the porch at eight o'clock, in his track pants and his Abercrombie & Fitch polo shirt. But before that he would have a job to do. We rose from our haunches and I caught the scruff of his neck and I led him along the aisles to the paint racks – Saturday-men watched, staff in yellow cover-alls watched, but no one approached us – and I showed him the white paint, how much of it there was and how cheap it was, and I explained I'd be pulling a spot check on the rain shelter at seven o'clock, sharp.

I let go of him then. I sucked up the last of my calm, and I said:

'Listen, Aodhan, we're doing a shopping run this afternoon . . . Can I fetch anything in particular? You two go for that barbecue salmon in the vac-packs, don't you?'

I left him ashen-faced and limp. I prowled the aisles some more and now these hot little barks of triumph came up as

I walked. The Saturday-men avoided my eyes, and they scurried from my path, and I barked a little louder. As I'm here, I thought, why not pick up a couple of things?

So I bought an extendable ladder and a claw hammer.

The automatic doors registered my presence at once and I was let outside to the sun-kissed afternoon. I propped and extended the ladder against the front of the store and I climbed with the claw hammer hanging coolly in my grip. It took no more than a half-dozen wrenches to loose the exclamation mark

!

from the Do-It-Rite and carefully I placed it under my arm – it was light as air – and I descended. I walked across the car park. I placed it carefully on the tarmac in front of the Volvo – my intention was to drive over it and smash it to pieces – but then I thought, no, that would be too quick. So I got down on my knees and I started to tap gently with the hammer at the blue plastic of the exclamation mark

!

until it began to crack here and there, and tiny shatter lines appeared, and these joined up, piece by piece, until the entire surface of the

!

had become a beautiful mosaic in the blue of the sign, like the trace of tiny backroads on an old map – marking out lost fields, lost kingdoms, a lost world – and I was serene as a bird riding the swells of morning air over those fields.

The squad car appeared.

FJORD OF KILLARY

So I bought an old hotel on the fjord of Killary. It was set hard by the harbour wall, with Mweelrea mountain across the water, and disgracefully grey skies above. It rained two hundred and eighty-seven days of the year, and the locals were given to magnificent mood swings. The night in question, the rain was particularly violent – it came down like handfuls of nails flung hard and fast by a seriously riled sky god. I was at this point eight months in the place and about convinced it would be the death of me.

'It's end-of-the-fucking-world stuff out there,' I said.

The chorus of locals in the hotel's lounge bar as always ignored me. I was a fretful blow-in, by their mark, and simply not cut out for tough, gnarly, west of Ireland living. They were listening, instead, to John Murphy, our alcoholic funeral director.

'I'll bury anythin' that fuckin' moves,' he said.

'Bastards, suicides, tinkers,' he said.

'I couldn't give a fuckin' monkey's,' he said.

Mweelrea is the most depressing mountain you've ever seen, by the way, and its gaunt, looming shape filled almost every view from the Water's Edge Hotel, the lounge bar's included. The locals drank mostly Bushmills whiskey and

Guinness stout, and they drank them to great excess. I wiped their slops from the counter with a bar cloth I had come to hate with a passion that verged on the insane. I said, 'But seriously, that's one motherfucker of a high tide, no?'

Barely the toss of a glance I received. The talk had shifted to roads, mileage, general directions. They made a geography of the country by the naming of pubs:

'Do you know Madigan's in Maynooth?'

'I do, of course.'

'You'd take a left there.'

'I have you now.'

The hotel had twenty-three bedrooms and listed westward. Set a can of peas on the floor of just about any bedroom and it would roll slowly in the direction of the gibbering Atlantic. The estate agent had gussied up the history of the place in the brochure – a traditional coaching inn, original beams, visited by Thackeray, heritage bleeding out the wazoo, etc. – and I had leapt at it. I was the last of the hopeless romantics.

The talk had moved on, briefly, from roads and directions.

'If he's still around when her bandages come off,' Bill Knott, the surveyor, said, 'he's a braver man than me.'

'Nice woman,' John Murphy agreed. 'As long as you don't put your hand in the cage.'

Behind the bar: the Guinness tap, the Smithwick's tap, the lager taps, the line of optics, the neatly stacked rows of glasses, and a high stool that sat by a wee slit of window that had a view across the water towards Mweelrea. The iodine tang of kelp hung in the air always, and put me in mind of embalming fluid. Bill Knott looked vaguely from his Bushmills towards the water.

'Highish alright,' he said. 'But now what'd we be talkin' about for Belmullet, would you say? Off a slow road?'

The primary interest of these people's lives, it often seemed, was how far one place was from another, and how long it might take to complete the journey, given the state of the roads. Bill had been in haulage as a young man and considered himself expert.

'I don't know, Bill,' I said.

'Would we say an hour twenty if you weren't tailbacked out of Newport?'

'I said I really don't fucking well know, Bill.'

'There are those'll say you'd do it in the hour.' He sipped, delicately. 'But you'd want to be grease fuckin' lightnin' coming up from Westport direction, wouldn't you?'

'We could be swimming it yet, Bill.'

I had made – despite it all – a mild success of myself in life. But on turning forty, the previous year, I had sensed exhaustion rising up in me, like rot. I found that to be alone with the work all day was increasingly difficult. And the city had become a jag on my nerves – there was too much young flesh around. The brochure about the hotel appeared in my life like a revelation. I clutched it in my hands for days on end. I grew feverish with the notion of a westward flight. I lay in bed with the brochure, as the throb of the city sounded a kind of raspy, taunting note, and I moaned as I read:

Original beams.

Traditional coaching inn.

Thackeray.

Estd 1648.

The hotel had the promise of an ideal solution. I could distract myself (from myself) with its day-to-day running, its endless small errands, and perhaps, late at night, or very early in the morning, I could continue, at some less intense level, with the poetry.

All my friends, every last one of them, said, 'The Shining'.

But I was thinking, the west of Ireland . . . the murmurous ocean . . . the rocky hills hard-founded in a greenish light . . . the cleansing air . . . the stoats peeping shyly from little gaps in the drystone walls . . .

Yes. It would all do to make a new man of me. Of course, I hadn't counted on having to listen to my summer staff, a pack of energetic young Belarusians, fucking each other at all angles of the clock.

And the ocean turned out to gibber rather than murmur.

Gibber gibber – whoosh. Gibber gibber – whoosh.

Down the far end of the bar, Mick Harty, distributor of bull semen for the vicinity, was molesting his enormously fat wife, Vivien.

'We're after a meal at the place run by the Dutch faggots,' he said. 'Oysters for a starter . . . They have me gone fuckin' bananas!'

Vivien slapped and roared at him as he stroked her massive haunches. She reddened and chortled as he twisted her around and pulled her vast rear side into his crotch area. Nobody apart from me paid a blind bit of attention to the spectacle. And even as she suffered a pretend butt-rape from her cackling husband, she turned to me and informed me, precisely, what they had paid for the meal at the Dutch couple's restaurant.

'Two starters, two mains, we shared a dessert, two bottles of wine, two cappuccinos,' she said, as Mick grinded slowly behind her, hoarsely yodelling an Alicia Keys love ballad. 'Hundred thirty-six euro, even – not cheap, Caoimhin.'

'Cappuccino is a breakfast drink,' I said. 'You're not supposed to drink it after a meal.'

I was not well liked out in Killary. I was considered 'superior'. Of course I was fucking superior. I ate at least five portions of fruit and veg daily. I had Omega 3 from oily fish coming out my ears. I limited myself to twenty-one units of alcohol a week. I hadn't written two consecutive lines of a poem in eight months. I was becoming versed, instead, in the strange, illicit practices of the hill country.

'Fuckers are washin' diesel up there again,' John Murphy said. 'The Hourigans? Of course, they'd a father a diesel-washer before 'em, didn't they? Cunts to a man.'

'Cunts,' Bill Knott confirmed.

Outside, the rain continued to hammer away at our dismal little world, and the sky had shucked the last of its evening grey to take on an intense purplish tone that was ominous, close-in, biblical.

'Sky is weirdin' up like I don't know fucking what,' I said.

John Murphy grabbed my elbow as I passed along the bar – he was aggressive, always, once the third pint was downed – and he said, 'I s'pose you know that possessed fuckin' she-devil above in the house will put me in the ground?'

'John,' I said, 'I really don't want to hear about it.'

'I mean literally, Caoimhin! She'll fuckin' do for me!'

'John, your marriage is your own private business.'

'She's fuckin' poisoning me! I swear to bleedin' fuckin' Jesus! I can taste it off the tea, Caoimh!'

'Would you go again, John?' I indicated his emptied stout glass.

'Oh, please,' he said.

They were all nutjobs. This is what it came down to. This is the thing you learn about habitual country drinkers.

'Mick's a man of sixty,' Vivien Harty said, awed at the persistence of her husband's desire, 'and he'd still get up on a cracked fuckin' plate.'

Just then a cacophony erupted:

From the hillsides, everywhere, came the aggravated howls of dogs. These were amped to an unnatural degree. The talk in the lounge bar stalled for a moment in response but, as abruptly, it resumed.

'The tiramisu?' Mick Harty said. 'You wouldn't know whether to eat it or smear it all over yourself.'

Nadia, one of my Belarusians, came through from the supper room and sullenly collected some glasses.

'The arse on that,' John Murphy said.

'Please, John,' I said.

'Two apples in a hankie,' he said.

I believed all nine of my staff to be in varying degrees of sexual contact with one another. I housed them in the dreary, viewless rooms at the back of the hotel, where I myself lived during what I will laughably describe as high season (the innocence), and my sleepless nights were filled with the sound of their rotating passions.

'Thank you, Nadia,' I said.

She scowled at me as she placed the glasses in the

dishwasher. I was never allowed to forget that I was paying minimum wage.

The dogs had stopped; the rain continued.

It was by now an hysterical downpour, with great sheets of water streaming down from Mweelrea, and the harbour roared in the fattening light. Visibility was reduced to fourteen feet. This all signalled that the west of Ireland holiday season had begun.

'He was thrun down,' John Murphy said, speaking of a man he had lately buried. 'He went into himself. He didn't talk for a year and a half and then he choked on a burnt rasher. You'd visit and he'd say nothin' to you but he'd know you were there all right. The little eyes would follow you around the room.'

'Age was he when he went, John?'

'Forty-two.'

'Youngish?'

'Arra. He was better off out of it.'

My first weeks out at the Water's Edge I had kept a surreptitious notebook under the bar. The likes of 'thrun down' would get a delighted entry. I would guess at the likely etymology – from 'thrown down', as in 'laid low'? But I had quickly had my fill of these maudlin bastards.

This, by the way, was the Monday of the May bank holiday weekend. Killary was *en fête*. Local opinion, cheerfully, was that it had been among the wettest bank holidays ever witnessed. The few deluded hillwalkers and cyclists who had shown up had departed early, in wordless outrage, and in the library room of the Water's Edge there was just a pair of elderly couples still enjoying the open fire. I left the bar and took a pass through the library to smile at them, throw on a few sods of turf, and to make sure they hadn't died on the premises.

They stared into the flames.

'That's some evening?' I tried, but there was no response.

Both couples held hands and appeared significantly tranquillised. Coming through the lobby again, I looked out through the doors and I saw a pair of minks creep over the harbour wall. They crossed the road, in perfect tandem, and headed for the rising fields beyond the hotel. I went back into the bar. I had an odd nausea developing.

'They can cut out that particular gland,' Bill Knott said, 'but if the wound goes septic after?'

He shook his head hopelessly.

'That,' he said, 'is when the fun and games start.'

Mine was one of four licensed premises in a scattered district of three-hundred-odd souls. This is a brutal scarcity, by Irish ratios, so there was enough trade to keep us all tunnelling towards oblivion. The bar was another of the elements that had sold the place to me. It was pleasant, certainly, with an old-fashioned mahogany finish, zinc-topped low tables, and some prints of photo finishes from fabled race meetings at Ballybrit. I always tended bar in the evenings. I'd had a deranged notion that this would establish me as a kind of charming-innkeeper figure. This was despite the fact that not one but two ex-girlfriends (both of them, admittedly, sharp-tongued academics) had described my manner as 'funereal'.

The bar-side babble continued unchecked:

Bill Knott was now reckoning the distance to Derry if

you were to go via Enniskillen. Vivien Harty was telling John Murphy that that wasn't tuppence worth of a coat his wife had on the Tuesday gone, that he was looking after her all the same, and that no woman deserved it more, given what she'd been through with the botched hysterectomy. Mick Harty talked of the cross-border trade in stallions and looked faintly murderous. 'Our horses the fuckers are after now,' he said.

Nadia, meantime, was singing weird Belarusian pop beneath her breath as she got up on the footstool to polish the optics. A seep of vomit rose in my gullet. I was soul sick. I was failing spectacularly at this whole mine-host lark. I quietly leaned on the bar by the till. I looked out the small window. Watery, it was.

'Seriously, lads, we haven't seen a tide that high, surely? Have we?'

It was lapping by now at the top of the harbour wall. The estate agent had assured me that the place never flooded. I'd looked the slithery old fuck in the eye and believed him. I had suspected, I had hoped, that the life I found out here would eventually do something for my work. Something would gestate in me. I'd be able to move away from all that obtuse, arrhythmic stuff about the sex heat of cities that had made me mildly famous in provincial English departments. My poetry was known of but was not a difficulty for the Killary locals – there had never been a shortage of poets out there. Every last crooked rock of the place had at some point seated the bony arse of some hypochondriacal epiphany-seeker. Some fucker who'd forever be giving out about his lungs.

'You'd do jail time for that,' John Murphy said.

He was eyeing once more the rear quarters of Nadia as she headed for the kitchen.

'John, I've warned you about this,' I said.

'I'm only sayin',' he said.

He sullenly turned back to his stout. The people of this part of north Galway are oversexed. That is my belief. I had found a level of ribaldry that bordered on the paganistic. It goes back, of course. They lick it up off the crooked rocks. Thackeray, indeed, remarked on the corset-less dress of rural Irish women, and the fact that they kissed perfect strangers in greeting, their vast bosoms swinging.

'It's not,' John Murphy said, 'like I'm goin' to take a lep at the little bitch. My leppin' days are long fuckin' over.'

A notion came: if I sold the place for even three-quarters of what I paid for it, I could buy half of Cambodia and do a Colonel fucking Kurtz on it altogether. Lovely, cold-hearted Nadia came running from the kitchen. She was as white as the fallen dead.

'Is otter!' she said.

'What?'

'Is otter in kitchen!' she said.

He was eating soup when I got there. Carrot and coriander from a ten-gallon pot. Normally, they are terribly skittish, otters, but this fellow was languorous as a surfer. Nervously, I shooed him towards the back door. He took his own sweet time about heading there. Once outside, he aimed not for the tide-line rocks, where the otters all lived, but for the higher ground, south.

I looked out towards the harbour. The harbour wall was

disappearing beneath spilling sheets of water. I came back into the lounge.

'A fucking otter is right,' I said.

They looked at me, the locals, in quiet disgust, as if I could expect no less than otters in the kitchen, the way I was after letting things go.

I pointed to the harbour.

'Will it flood?' I asked, and there was a quake in my tone.

'You'd make good time coming out of Sligo, normally,' Bill Knott said. 'Unless you had a Thursday on your hands. But of course them fuckers have any amount of road under them since McSharry was minister.'

'I said will it flood, Bill? Will it flood? Are you even listening to me?'

A grey silence swelled briefly.

'Hasn't in sixteen years,' he said. 'Won't now.'

I spent all my waking hours keeping the Water's Edge on the go. I was short-breathed, tense, out of whack. I was at roughly the midpoint of what, for poets, would be termed 'a long silence' – five years had passed since my last collection. Anytime I sat down to page or screen, I felt as if I might weep, and I didn't always resist the temptation. Mountain bleakness, the lapidary rhythms of the water, the vast schizophrenic skies: these weren't inspiring poetry in me; they were inspiring hopeless lust and negative thought patterns. Again and again, the truth was confronting me – I was a born townie, and I had made a dreadful mistake in coming here. I set down a fresh Bushmills for Bill Knott.

'This place your crowd are from,' he said. 'Belarus?'

'Yes, Bill?'

'What way'd they be for road out there?'

'When you think,' Vivien Harty said, 'of what this country went through for the sake of Europe, when we went on our hands and fuckin' knees before Brussels, to be given the lick of a fuckin' butter voucher, and as soon as we have ourselves even halfways right, these bastards from the back end of nowhere decide they can move in wherever they like and take our fuckin' jobs?'

On the Killary hillsides the dogs howled again in fright-night sequence, one curdling scream giving way to another; they were even louder now than before.

'Mother of Jesus,' John Murphy said.

The dogs were so loud now as to be unignorable. We all went to the windows. The roadway between hotel and harbour wall had in recent moments disappeared. The last of the evening light was an unreal throb of Kermit green. The dogs howled. The rain continued.

'The roads,' Bill Knott said, at last impressed, 'will be unpassable.'

Mick Harty's hands slipped down over the backs of Vivien's thighs. The rain came in great, unstoppable drifts on a high westerly from the Atlantic.

'That ain't quittin' anytime soon,' I said, stating the blindingly obvious.

'Water's up to the second step,' Vivien Harty noted.

Four old stone steps led up to the inn's front porch.

'And rising,' Mick Harty said.

'I haven't seen rain the likes of that,' John Murphy said, 'since Castlebar, the March of 'seventy-three.'

'What'd we be talkin' about for Castlebar?' Bill Knott said. 'Forty-five minutes on a light road?'

*

We moved back from the windows. Our movement had become curiously choreographed. Quiet calls were made on mobiles. We spoke now in whispers.

All along the fjord, word quickly had it, the waters had risen and had breached the harbour walls. The emergency services had been alerted. There was talk – a little late for it – of sandbagging. We were joined in the lounge bar by six of the nine Belarusians – the other three had gone to the cineplex in Westport, fate having put on a Dan Brown adaptation – and by the two elderly couples, who had managed not to die off in the library.

I said, 'A round of drinks on the house, folks. We may be out here for some time.'

Applause greeted this. I felt suddenly that I was growing into the mine-host role. There was a conviviality in the bar now, the type that is said to come always with threatened disaster.

Great howls of wind echoed down the Doo Lough Valley, and they were answered in volleyed sequence by the howls of the Killary dogs.

Four of the six Belarusians wore love bites on their necks as they sipped at their complimentary bottled Heinekens. They were apparently feasting delightedly on each other in my back rooms.

The elderlies introduced themselves.

We met Alan and Norah Fettle from Limerick, and Jimmy and Janey McAllister from Limavady. They were the least scared among us, the least awed.

'Yon wind's changing,' Jimmy Mac said. 'Yon wind's shiftin' easterly so 'tis.'

'I wouldn't like the sounds of that,' John Murphy said.

'Not much good will come ever out of a swappin' wind. You'd hear that said.'

It was said also in Killary that an easterly wind unseated the mind.

I shot a glance outside, and on a low branch of the may tree hanging over the water a black-backed gull had apparently killed its mate and was starting to eat it. This didn't seem like news that anybody wanted to hear, so I kept it to myself.

Alexei, the conspicuously wall-eyed Belarusian, had gone to survey the scene from an upstairs window and he returned to report that the car park beside the hotel was flooded completely.

'Insurance will cover any damage,' Bill Knott soothed.

'It's going to be one of those fuckin' news clips,' John Murphy said. 'Some fuckin' ape sailin' down the street on a tea tray.'

'Jesus Christ what's that gull doing?' Norah Fettle said.

It was an inopportune moment to draw attention to the gull situation. The black-back had just at that instant managed to prise its partner's head off, and was flailing it about. Janey McAllister passed out cold on the floor. There was no getting away from the fact that we were being sucked into the deeps of an emergency.

I was getting happy notions. I was thinking, the place gets wiped out, I claim the insurance, and it's Cambodia here I come.

Norah Fettle and Vivien Harty tended to Janey McAllister. She was frothing a little, and moaning softly. They called for brandy. Bill Knott signalled for a fresh Bushmills, John Murphy for a pint of stout.

We all looked out the windows.

The water had passed the fourth step and was sweeping over the porch. We were on some vague level aware that house lights still burned on the far side of the harbour, along the mountainside of Mweelrea. Then, at once, the lights over there cut out.

'Good night, Irene,' Bill Knott said.

The worst of the news was that the emergency appeared to be localised. The fjord of Killary was flooding when no other place was flooding. The rest of the country was going about its humdrum Monday-night business – watching football matches, or Dan Brown adaptations, putting out the bins, or putting up with their marriages – while the people of our vicinity prepared for watery graves.

I felt the worst possible course would be to close the bar. There was a kind of hilarity to the proceedings still, and this would not be maintained if I stopped serving booze. The pace of the drinking, if anything, quickened now that the waters were rising. You never know when you are going to lift your last.

'Would we want to be making south?' Mick Harty wondered.

Vivien rubbed at his wrist so tenderly I found myself welling up.

'Hush,' she said. 'Hush it, babes.'

'If we went up past Lough Fee and swung around the far side of her,' Bill Knott said, 'we'd nearly make it to the N59.'

The Belarusians carted boxloads of old curtains from the attic to use as sops against the doorways but the moment the last boxload reached the bottom of the stairs the doors popped and the waters of Killary entered.

I moved everybody upstairs. There was a function room up there that I used for the occasional wedding. It had a fully stocked bar and operational disco lights. We weren't a moment too soon. As I trailed up the stairs, keeping to the rear of all my locals and Belarusians, I cast an eye back over my shoulder. It had the look of death's dateless night out there.

'Hup, people!' I cried. 'Hup for Jesus' sake!'

More calls were made on mobiles. We were promised that the emergency services were being moved out. I turned off the harsh strip lighting overhead and switched to the mood lighting, which moved in lovely, dreamy, disco swirls. Even yet the rain hammered down on my old hotel at Killary. I opened the bar, and the locals weren't shy about stepping up to it.

We drank.

We whispered.

We laughed like cats.

Bill Knott reckoned the distance to Clare Island oversea, if it should come to it.

'Of course, it would not be the first time,' he said, 'that the likes of us would be sent hoppin' for the small boats.'

Vivien Harty whispered to Janey McAllister. Janey's colour was returning with frequent nips of my brandy. Vivien swirled it in the glass and fed it to the old lady; her tiny grey head she cradled on a vast lap.

Thackeray, on visiting the backwoods of Ireland, bemoaned the 'choking peat smoke' and the 'obstreperous cider' and the diet of 'raw ducks, raw pease' and also a particular inn: 'No pen can describe that establishment, as no English imagination could have conceived it.'

John Murphy told us, loudly, that he loved his wife.

'She still excites me,' he said. 'It's been twenty-eight years, and I still get a horn on me when I see that bitch climb a stairs.'

I went to the landing outside the function room. I looked down the road. It was a waterway; the hotel porch had disappeared, and dozens of cormorants were approaching in formation across the water. It was like the attack on Dresden. I rushed back to the function room just as the cormorants landed on the kitchen roof out back, and a weeping Mick Harty was confessing to Vivien an affair of fifteen years' standing. With her sister.

'All the auld filth starts to come out,' Alan Fettle said.

Vivien approached her husband, and embraced him, and planted a light kiss on his neck as they held each other against the darkness. Then she bit him on the neck. Blood came in great, angry spurts. I vomited, briefly, and decided to put on some music.

I looked out the landing window as I dashed along the corridor to get some CDs from my room – this was a bad move:

Seven sheep in a rowing boat were being bobbed about on the vicious waters of Killary. The sheep appeared strangely calm.

I picked lots of old familiars: Abba, The Pretenders, Bryan Adams.

I pelted back to the function room.

'We're here!' I cried. 'We might as well have a disco!'

Oh, and we danced the night away out on the fjord of Killary. We danced to 'Chiquitita', slowly and sensuously; we danced in great, wet-eyed nostalgia to 'Brass in Pocket', and we had all the old steps still, as if 1979 was only yesterday; we punched the air madly to 'Summer of '69'.

I went out to the landing to find the six Belarusians sitting on the top step of the stairs. The waters of Killary were halfway up the stairs. Footstools sailed by in the lobby below, toilet rolls, place mats, phone books. But what could I do?

I returned to the function room and served out pints hand over fist.

All mobile signals were down.

There appeared on the horizon no saviours in hi-viz clothing.

The waters were rising yet.

And the view was suddenly clear to me. The world opened out to its grim beyonds and I realised that, at forty, one must learn the rigours of acceptance. Capitalise it: Acceptance. I needed to accept what was put before me – be it a watery grave in Ireland's only natural fjord, or a return to the city and its greyer intensities, or a wordless exile in some steaming Cambodian swamp hole, or poems or no poems, or children or not, lovers or not, illness or otherwise, success or its absence. I would accept all that was put in my way, from here on through until I breathed my last.

Electrified, I searched for a notebook.

Bill Knott danced. John Murphy danced. The McAllisters and the Fettles waltzed. The Belarusians dry-humped one another in the function room's dark corners. The Hartys were in deep, emotional conversation in a booth – Mick held to his bleeding neck a wad of napkins. I myself took to the floor, swivelling slowly on my feet, and I closed my eyes against the swirling lights. The pink backs of my eyelids became twin screens for flashing apparitions of my childhood pets.

'Are ye enjoyin' yereselves, lads?'

'What would we be talkin' about for Loughrea, would you say?'

'Didn't I come back from that place one lung half the size of the other?'

'That's England for you.'

I ran out to the landing for a spot check on the flood, and was met there by Alexei, the wall-eyed Belarusian. He indicated with a happy jerk of his thumb the water level on the stairs. It had dropped a couple of steps. I patted his back, and winked just the once, and returned to the disco.

1648 was a year shy of Cromwell's landing in Ireland, and already the inn at Killary fjord was in business – it would see out this disaster, too. Now random phrases and images came at me – the sudden quick-fire assaults that signal a new idea – and I knew that they would come in sequence soon enough, their predestined rhythms would assert. I felt a new, quiet ecstasy take hold.

The gloom of youth had at last lifted.

A CRUELTY

He climbs the twenty-three steps of the metal traverse bridge at 9.25 a.m., and not an instant before. Boyle station, a grey and blowy summer's day. He counts each step as he climbs, the ancient rusted girders of the bridge clamped secure with enormous bolts, and the way the roll of his step is a fast plimsoll shuffle as he crosses – the stride is determined, the arms are swinging – and he counts off the twenty-three steps that descend again to the far-side platform. The clanky bamp of the last metal step gives way to a softer footfall on the platform's smooth aged stone, and the surge of the Dublin–Sligo train comes distantly, but now closer, and now at a great building roar along the track – the satisfaction of timing it just right – and the train's hot breeze unsettles his hair. The train eases to a halt, and his hair fixes; the doors beep three times and airily hiss open: an expectant gasp. He takes his usual place in carriage A. There is no question of a ticket being needed but the inspector sticks his head into the carriage anyway to bid a good morning.

'That's not a bad-looking day at all,' Donie says.

It is his joke to say this in all weathers. He said it throughout the great freeze of Christmas and the year's turn, he said it during the floods of November '09. Now a roar comes out of the north, also, and the Sligo–Dublin train pulls in alongside, and its noise deflates, with the passengers boredly staring – it is at Boyle station always that the trains keep company, for a few minutes, and for Donie this is a matter of pride. Boyle is a town happily fated, he believes, a place where things of interest will tend to happen.

The beeps and the hissing, the carriages are sealed, and the Dublin train heads off for Connolly station, but Donie's train does not yet move. The schedule declares his train will leave for Sligo at 9.33 a.m. and he becomes anxious now as he watches the seconds tick by on his Casio watch.

9.33.35

9.33.36

9.33.37

And when the seconds ascend into the fifties, his breath starts to come in hard panicked stabs of anxiety, and he speaks.

'We'd want to be making a move here, lads,' he says.

It is a painful twenty-eight seconds into 9.34 a.m. when the train drags up its great power from within, and the doors close again and the departure is made.

Why, Donie demands, when the train has had a full eight minutes to wait on the platform, can it not leave precisely at the appointed time of its schedule?

'There is no call for it,' he says.

And it is not as if his watch is out – no fear – for he checks it each morning against the speaking clock. The speaking clock is a state-run service; it surely cannot be wrong. If it was, the whole system would be thrown out.

The train climbs to the high ground outside Boyle. He

rides the ascent into the Curlew mountains, and he whistles past the graveyard. The judder and surge of the engine is its usual excitement and he tries to forget the anxiety of Boyle station, but it recedes slowly as tide. Now the broken-down stone walls of the old rising fields. Now the mournful cows still wet from the dew and night's drizzle. Now the greenish tone of the galvanised tin roof on the lost shack. The spits of rain against the window, and the high looming of the Bricklieves on a mid-distant rise, north-westerly, a smooth-cut limestone plateau.

He was allowed to make the journey first on the morning of his sixteenth birthday. This is now the twentieth year of his riding the Boyle–Sligo leg, all the working days of the week, all the weeks of the year. It is Donie's belief that if he is not on the 9.33 train, the 9.33 will not run, and who is there to say otherwise?

And distantly, now, the iridescence of the lakes, a vapourish glow rising beyond the hills, and the father is dead of the knees. The father was a great walker and he walked five miles daily a loop of the Lough Key forest park, among the ferns and the ancient oaks, across the fairy bridge and back again. Then the knees went on the father – the two simultaneously – and he could walk no more.

'Oh I have a predicament now,' he would say from the armchair, looking out at Boyle; the slow afternoons.

The weight piled up on the father quickly. He turned into a churn of butter on the armchair. He took a heart attack inside the year.

'My father,' Donie tells people, 'died of a predicament of the knees.'

The high land of the south county. The approach to

Ballymote. He names the fields for the elder, the yellow iris (the flags), the dog rose. Past the hill of Keash – a marker – and it is 9.45 a.m. on the nose, the lost seconds have been regained; the breath runs easily the length of Donie again. High above the treetops the tower of the castle of Ballymote appears, it is worried this morning by rooks, the rooks blown about on the fresh summer breezes; the rooks are at their play up there. Two elderly ladies wait on the Ballymote platform and Donie knows they are for the Sligo hospital – he can see the sickness in them; they are gaunt and drawn from its creeping spread.

He rides the descent to Collooney. He wills it along the track. Collooney is the last stop before Sligo and as always an encumbrance – he is anxious again; he wants this stop done with; the train must hit Sligo town on the clock. If the time is out, he will know it is out, and it will be an aggravation. Collooney brings on three passengers and he cannot help but mutter at them as they move along the aisle.

'Ye'd be as quick to get the bus, lads,' he says.

Sea's hint on the air, and the surge of the motorway beside, and it is the gulls that are flung about now on the breeze, and the back gardens of the terrace houses are a peripheral blur – unpainted fences, the coiled green of hoses, breezeblock – and his eyes water they are focused so hard on the seconds of the Casio watch . . .

10.08.53
10.08.54
10.08.55

. . . and he knows it is all to the good now, as the train eases into the station, as its surge diminishes, and dies.

10.09.15 – the arrival has been made within the named minute of the schedule, and there is a lightness to Donie's step as he walks out through the station; the stride is jaunty, the arms again swinging.

It is time to head down to the Garavogue river and have a check on the ducks.

Where the river breaches before the bridge, the current is quick and vicious. Often here, in summer, a mallard fledgling is swept away from its brood, and more than once Donie has climbed down the stone steps – one careful plimsoll at a time to gauge each step for slickness – and he has made it with great trepidation across the rocks where the water diverges, and more than one family he has remade, the tiny damp fowl held carefully in his hands. On a morning two years ago, schoolgirls applauded as Donie went about his work. The delicate thrum of life fluttered within his cupped palms.

This morning, all seems to be flowing well enough, but he keeps an eye on things, duck-wise, for the full half-hour anyway.

Now the satchel.

Donie has taught himself to ignore the presence of the satchel on his back until quarter to eleven precisely. If he does not, the sandwiches and the biscuits will not survive even the train journey. He sits on a bench further along the riverside than his usual bench but it is not a major annoyance. Often enough, the usual bench is taken, especially on a summer morning, and he is resigned to the fact. It just means that this will not be a 100 per cent day, a day when everything falls into place just as it should. A sadness but a mild one.

From the satchel he takes first the larger of the foil packages and carefully unpicks the ends of the foil and releases the warm smell of the bread. Two sandwiches, halved, of white bread, ham, spread, and nothing else. When it comes to sandwiches, Donie is straight down the line. No messing.

Would ye go 'way with yere coleslaw, he thinks, and cheerfully he lifts the first plain bite to his mouth.

The sandwiches are washed down with the bottle of orange. The orange is followed by the four biscuits wrapped also in foil. For a while, the biscuits would vary – if only for variety's sake, was the mother's reasoning – but the variance threw Donie out. It became an agitation to him that he did not know whether it would be fig rolls or Hobnobs he was getting. He could guess accurately enough by shape but there'd come a morning of round biscuits and who was to tell a Chocolate Goldgrain from a Polo? It was a dead loss, and it is specified now that it is Chocolate Goldgrain he will unwrap.

He has just finished the last of the biscuits when someone sits down beside. Donie needn't look up to know that eyes are on him – the heat of a stare burns like nettle sting across every inch of his flesh.

'How're we?' the man says.

Donie raises his glance now and finds a man wearing a thin, half-grown beard, and he is pale-eyed, and yellowish of the flesh.

'What's it they call you?' the man says.

'Donie.'

'Ah yeah. Is it short for Domhnaill?'

'It is.'

'The Irish spelling?'

'That's right. D.O.M.H . . .'

'Good . . .'

'N.A.I.L.L.'

'*Very* good. Give the boy a biscuit.'

'I ate my last biscuit.'

'It's an expression, you poor dumb cunt.'

Donie knows that he must rise and go but the man reaches across and lays a steel-cold hand on his. Clamps it to the bench.

'Stop that,' Donie says.

The man giggles.

'I'd say the best part of Donie dribbled down the father's leg, did it?'

The thin hard bones of the hand, the yellow of the skin . . . there is something the man brings to mind but Donie cannot place it specifically. He knows that there is the sensation of an animal.

'I've to go now,' Donie says.

'If you get up I'll kick the ankles out from under you.'

'Don't do that!'

Donie's voice quakes and the words are tiny and lost almost to the roar of the river.

'He's sobbing!'

Donie looks at the man's hand locked on his and the yellow of the spots on the back of the man's hand and it comes to him, the word comes from the colouring: hyena.

'You're like a hyena,' he says.

The man whistles a laugh down his nose. Another comes in quick succession. He shakes with thin hilarity. He continues to lock Donie's hand to the bench but now moves his thumb slowly and sensuously along the back of the hand.

'Don't.'

'Why?'

'It tiddles.'

'And what would a hyena do to you, Donie?'

'Will you leave me go now?'

'What would he do? A hyena?'

'I have to go home to my mother. I have the twelve o'clock train to get.'

'Would it have a feed off your corpse, would you say?'

'I get the twelve o'clock to Boyle station. It gets in 12.33 p.m.'

'Take tiny little bites, would it?'

The man grinds and bites with his teeth rapidly – he gnashes, and he aims a sharp smile at Donie.

'Will we go for a walk so?' he says.

Donie with all the force he can muster wrenches his hand free and rises from the bench to go. The man is up as quickly, and as he walks beside Donie, he places a hand softly on his lower back, and he whispers super-fast the bad words now.

'Do you know what I'll do to you when I see you down here again . . .' is how it begins but the rest is lost to the high-vaulted pitch of Donie's screech. The screech is held as a shield against the words. But the man just gently shushes.

'Easy now, honey-child,' he says.

The man stops suddenly, and Donie feels the hand lift from his back, and he feels the dread of the pause, and now there is a piston jerk of force from opened palm to small of back, and the man sticks a leg out to trip Donie as he flails forward, and he is sprawled on the pathway by the riverside and there are people all about, but nobody comes forward to help. Donie knows they think it's just mad fellas fighting.

He is on the ground and the man is for a moment above him, is blocking out the sky, and he leans down close.

'Hyena,' he says, and walks away.

All is thrown out for Donie now as he goes through the tight streets of Sligo town. He does not stop today to look at the equipment in the mountaineering shop, and usually that is a fifteen-minute dream for Donie, a dream of crampons and frost-in-the-beard and great snowy peaks. He does not today say hello to the wood carver. He does not count the paving slabs through the arcade shortcut.

An hour is lost to trembles on the platform. And he is sat on the twelve o'clock train now but he misses its departure utterly as the eyes of the hyena burn into him. He misses Collooney and the climb to Ballymote. He has no joke for the inspector. The high land of the south county; hyena. The lost shack, and he does not today fantasise the happy family that once lived there. Boyle station; hyena.

'What's up with you, Donie?'

A kind man notes the distress and says the words on Elphin Road in the town of Boyle but Donie does not stop to talk to him. He does not go to Supervalu for the bag of six donuts. He goes straight back to the terrace.

The sun has come out. It is a pure white screech of sun. He hurries along the row of houses as familiar as the mouth-feel of his own teeth and he must squint into the sun, into

54

the light, and the feeling does not break and it will not ease – hyena – until the door of the house opens for him, and it does so, and she steps outside, the moment timed to his arrival, her silhouette against the glare of the sun, mother-shaped.

BEER TRIP TO LLANDUDNO

It was a pig of a day, as hot as we'd had, and we were down to our T-shirts taking off from Lime Street. This was a sight to behold – we were all of us biggish lads. It was Real Ale Club's July outing, a Saturday, and we'd had word of several good houses to be found in Llandudno. I was double-jobbing for Ale Club that year. I was in charge of publications and outings both. Which was controversial.

'Rhyl . . . We'll pass Rhyl, won't we?'

This was Mo.

'We'd have come over to Rhyl as kids,' said Mo. 'Ferry and coach. I remember the rollercoasters.'

'Never past Prestatyn, me,' said Tom Neresford.

Tom N – so-called; there were three Toms in Ale Club – rubbed at his belly in a worried way. There was sympathy for that. We all knew stomach trouble for a bugger.

'Down on its luck'd be my guess,' said Everett Bell. 'All these old North Wales resorts have suffered dreadfully, haven't they? Whole mob's gone off to bloody Laos on packages. Bloody Cambodia, bucket and spade.'

Everett wasn't inclined to take the happy view of things. Billy Stroud, the ex-Marxist, had nothing to offer about Llandudno. Billy was involved with his timetables.

'Two minutes and fifty seconds late taking off,' he said,

as the train skirted the Toxteth estates. 'This thing hits Llandudno for 1.55 p.m., I'm an exotic dancer.'

Aigburth station offered a clutch of young girls in their summer skimpies. Oiled flesh, unscarred tummies, and it wasn't yet noon. We groaned under our breaths. We'd taken on a crate of Marston's Old Familiar for the journey, 3.9 per cent to volume. Outside, the estuary sulked away in terrific heat and Birkenhead shimmered across the water. Which wasn't like Birkenhead. I opened my *AA Illustrated Guide to Britain's Coast* and read from its entry on Llandudno:

'A major resort of the North Wales coastline, it owes its well-planned streets and promenade to one Edward Mostyn, who, in the mid-19th century –'

'Victorian effort,' said John Mosely. 'Thought as much.'

If there was a dad figure among us, it was Big John, with his know-it-all interruptions.

'Who, in the mid-19th century,' I repeated, 'laid out a new town on former marshland below . . .'

'They've built it on a marsh, have they?' said Everett Bell.

'TB,' said Billy Stroud. 'Marshy environment was considered healthful.'

'Says here there's water skiing available from Llandudno jetty.'

'That'll be me,' said Mo, and we all laughed.

Hot as pigs, but companionable, and the train was in Cheshire quick enough. We had dark feelings about Cheshire that summer. At the North West Beer Festival, in the spring, the Cheshire crew had come over a shade cocky. Just because they were chocka with half-beam pubs in pretty villages. Warrington lads were fine. We could take the Salford lot even. But the Cheshire boys were arrogant and we sniffed as we passed through their country.

'A bloody suburb, essentially,' said Everett.

'Chester's a regular shithole,' said Mo.

'But you'd have to allow Delamere Forest is a nice walk?' said Tom N.

Eyebrows raised at this, Tom N not being an obvious forest walker.

'You been lately, Tom? Nice walk?'

Tom nodded, all sombre.

'Was out for a Christmas tree, actually,' he said.

This brought gales of laughter. It is strange what comes over as hilarious when hangovers are general. We had the windows open to circulate what breeze there was. Billy Stroud had an earpiece in for the radio news. He winced:

'They're saying it'll hit 36.5,' he said. 'Celsius.'

We sighed. We sipped. We made Wales quick enough and we raised our Marston's to it. Better this than to be stuck in a garden listening to a missus. We meet as much as five nights of the week, more often six. There are those who'd call us a bunch of sots but we don't see ourselves like that. We see ourselves as hobbyists. The train pulled into Flint and Tom N went on the platform to fetch in some beef 'n' gravies from the Pie-O-Matic.

'Just the thing,' said Billy Stroud, as we sweated over our dripping punnets. 'Cold stuff causes the body too much work, you feel worse. But a nice hot pie goes down a treat. Perverse, I know. But they're on the curries in Bombay, aren't they?'

'Mumbai,' said Everett.

The train scooted along the fried coast. We made solid headway into the Marston's. Mo was down a testicle since the spring. We'd called in at the Royal the night of his operation. We'd stopped at the Ship and Mitre on the way – they'd a handsome bitter from Clitheroe on guest tap. We needed the fortification: when Real Ale Club boys parade down hospital wards, we tend to draw worried glances from the whitecoats. We are shaped like those chaps in the warning illustrations on cardiac charts. We gathered around Mo and breathed a nice fog of bitter over the lad and we joshed him but gently.

'Sounding a little high-pitched, Mo?'

'Other lad's going to be worked overtime.'

'Diseased bugger you'll want in a glass jar, Mo. One for the mantelpiece.'

Love is a strong word, but. We were family to Mo when he was up the Royal having the bollock out. We passed Flint Castle and Everett Bell piped up.

'Richard the Second,' he said.

We raised eyebrows. We were no philistines at Ale Club, Merseyside branch. Everett nodded, pleased.

'This is where he was backed into a corner,' he said. 'By Bolingbroke.'

'Boling who?'

'Bolingbroke, the usurper. Old Dick surrendered for a finish. At Flint Castle. Or that's how Shakespeare had it.'

'There's a contrary view, Ev?'

'Some say it was more likely Conwy but I'd be happy with the Bard's read,' he said, narrowing his eyes, the matter closed.

'We'll pass Conwy Castle in a bit, won't we?'

I consulted my *Illustrated AA*.

'We'll not,' I said. 'But we may well catch a glimpse across the estuary from Llandudno Junction.'

There was a holiday air at the stations. Families piled on, the dads with papers, the mams with lotion, the kids with phones. The beer ran out by Abergele and this was frowned upon: poor planning. We were reduced to buying train beer, Worthington's. Sourly we sipped and Everett came and had a go.

'Maybe if one man wasn't in charge of outings *and* publications,' he said, 'we wouldn't be running dry halfways to Llandudno.'

'True, Everett,' I said, calmly, though I could feel the colour rising to my cheeks. 'So if anyone cares to step up, I'll happily step aside. From either or.'

'We need you on publications, kid,' said John Mosely. 'You're the man for the computers.'

Publications lately was indeed largely web-based. I maintained our site on a regular basis, posting beer-related news and links. I was also looking into online initiatives to attract the younger drinker.

'I'm happy on publications, John,' I said. 'The debacle with the newsletter aside.'

Newsletter had been a disaster, I accepted that. The report on the Macclesfield outing had been printed upside down. Off-colour remarks had been made about a landlady in Everton, which should never have got past an editor's eye, as the lady in question kept very fine pumps. It hadn't been for want of editorial meetings. We'd had several, mostly down the Grapes of Wrath.

'So how's about outings then?' I said, as the train swept

by Colwyn Bay. 'Where's our volunteer there? Who's for the step-up?'

Everett showed a palm to placate me.

'There's nothin' personal in this, lad,' he said.

'I know that, Ev.'

Ale Club outings were civilised events. They never got aggressive. Maudlin, yes, but never aggressive. Rhos-on-Sea; the Penrhyn sands. We knew Everett had been through a hard time. His old dad passed on and there'd been sticky business with the will. Ev would turn a mournful eye on us, at the bar of the Lion, in the snug of the Ship, and he'd say:

'My brother got the house, my sister got the money, I got the manic depression.'

Black as his moods could be, as sharp as his tongue, Everett was tender. Train came around Little Ormes Head and Billy Stroud went off on one about Ceauşescu.

'Longer it recedes in the mind's eye,' he said, 'the more like Romania seems the critical moment.'

'Apropos of, Bill?'

'Apropos my arse. As for Liverpool? Myth was piled upon myth, wasn't it? They said Labour sent out termination notices to council workers by taxi. Never bloody happened! It was an anti-red smear!'

'Thatcher's sick and old, Billy,' said John Mosely.

'Aye an' her spawn's all around us yet,' said Billy, and he broke into a broad smile, his humours mysteriously righted, his fun returned.

Looming, then, the shadow of Great Ormes Head, and beneath it a crescent swathe of bay, a beach, a prom, and terraces: here lay Llandudno.

'1.55 p.m.,' said Everett. 'On the nose.'

'Where's our exotic dancer?' teased Mo.

Billy Stroud sadly raised his T-shirt above his man boobs. He put his arms above his head and gyrated slowly his vast belly and danced his way off the train. We lost weight in tears as we tumbled onto the platform.

'How much for a private session, miss?' called Tom N.

'Tenner for twenty minutes,' said Billy. 'Fiver, I'll stay the full half-hour.'

We walked out of Llandudno station and plumb into a headbutt of heat.

'Blood and tar!' I cried. 'We'll be hittin' the lagers!'

'Wash your mouth out with soap and water,' said John Mosely.

Big John rubbed his hands together and led the way – Big John was first over the top. He reminded us there was business to hand.

'We're going to need a decision,' he said, 'about the National Beer Scoring System.'

Here was kerfuffle. The NBSS, by long tradition, ranked a beer from nought to five. Nought was take-backable, a crime against the name of ale. One was barely drinkable, two so-so, three an eyebrow raised in mild appreciation. A four was an ale on top form, a good beer in proud nick. A five was angel's tears but a seasoned drinker would rarely dish out a five, would over the course of a lifetime's quaffing call no more than a handful of fives. Such was the NBSS, as was. However, Real Ale Club, Merseyside branch, had for some time felt that the system lacked subtlety. And one famous night, down Rigby's, we came up with our own system – we marked from nought to ten. Finer gradations of purity were thus allowed for. The nuances of a beer were more properly considered. A certain hoppy tang, redolent of summer hedgerows, might elevate a brew from a seven to an eight. The mellow back-note born of a good oak casking might lift an ale again, and to the rare peaks of the nines. Billy Stroud had argued for decimal breakdown, for 7.5s and 8.5s – Billy would – but we had to draw a line somewhere. The national organisation responded badly. They sent stiff word down the email but we continued to forward our beer reports with markings on a nought to ten scale. There was talk now of us losing the charter. These were heady days.

'Stuff them is my view,' said Everett Bell.

'We'd lose a lot if we lost the charter,' said Mo. 'Think about the festival invites. Think about the history of the branch.'

'Think about the bloody future!' cried Tom N. 'We haven't come up with a new system to be awkward. We've done it for the ale drinkers. We've done it for the ale makers!'

I felt a lump in my throat and I daresay I wasn't alone.

'Ours is the better system,' said Everett. 'This much we know.'

'You're right,' said John Mosely, and this was the clincher, Big John's call. 'I say we score nought to ten.'

'If you lot are in, that's good enough for me,' I said.

Six stout men linked arms on a hot Llandudno pavement. We rounded the turn onto the prom and our first port of call: the Heron Inn.

Which turned out to be an anti-climax. A nice house, lately refurbished, but mostly keg rubbish on the taps. The

Heron did, however, do a Phoenix Tram Driver on cask, 3.8 per cent, and we sat with six of same.

'I've had better Tram Drivers,' opened Mo.

'I've had worse,' countered Tom N.

'She has a nice delivery but I'd worry about her legs,' said Billy Stroud, shrewdly.

'You wouldn't be having more than a couple,' said John Mosely.

'*Not* a skinful beer,' I concurred.

All eyes turned to Everett Bell. He held a hand aloft, wavered it.

'A five would be generous, a six insane,' he said.

'Give her the five,' said Big John, dismissively.

I made the note. This was as smoothly as a beer was ever scored. There had been some world-historical ructions in our day. There was the time Billy Stroud and Mo hadn't talked for a month over an eight handed out to a Belhaven Bombardier.

Alewards we followed our noses. We walked by the throng of the beach – the shrieks of the sun-crazed kids made our stomachs loop. We made towards the Prom View Hotel. We'd had word of a new landlord there an ale-fancier. It was dogs-dying-in-parked-cars weather. The Prom View's ample lounge was a blessed reprieve. We had the place to ourselves, the rest of Llandudno apparently being content with summer, sea and life. John Mosely nodded towards a smashing row of hand pumps for the casks. Low whistles sounded. The landlord, hot-faced and jovial, came through from the hotel's reception.

'Another tactic,' he said, 'would be stay home and have a nice sauna.'

'Same difference,' sighed John Mosely.

'Could be looking at 37.2 now,' said the landlord, taking a flop of sweat from his brow.

Billy Stroud sensed a kindred spirit:

'Gone up again, has it?'

'And up,' said the landlord. 'My money's on a 38 before we're out.'

'Record won't go,' said Billy.

'Nobody's said record,' said the landlord. 'We're not going to see a 38.5, that's for sure.'

'Brogdale in Kent,' said Billy. 'August 10th, 2003.'

'2.05 p.m.,' said the landlord. 'I wasn't five miles distant that same day.'

Billy was beaten.

'Loading a van for a divorced sister,' said the landlord, ramming home his advantage. 'Lugging sofas in the piggin' heat. And wardrobes!'

We bowed our heads to the man.

'What'll I fetch you, gents?'

A round of Cornish Lightning was requested.

'Taking the sun?' enquired the landlord.

'Taking the ale.'

'After me own heart,' he said. ''Course 'round here, it's lagers they're after mostly. Bloody Welsh.'

'Can't beat sense into them,' said John Mosely.

'If I could, I would,' said the landlord, and he danced as a young featherweight might, he raised his clammy dukes. Then he skipped and turned.

'I'll pop along on my errands, boys,' he said. 'There are rows to hoe and socks for the wash. You'd go through pair after pair this weather.'

He pinched his nostrils closed: what-a-pong.

'Soon as you're ready for more, ring that bell and my good wife will oblige. So adieu, adieu . . .'

He skipped away. We raised eyes. The shade of the lounge was pleasant, the Cornish Lightning in decent nick.

'Call it a six?' said Tom N.

Nervelessly we agreed. Talk was limited. We swallowed hungrily, quickly, and peered again towards the pumps.

'The Lancaster Bomber?'

'The Whitstable Mule?'

'How's about that Mangan's Organic?'

'I'd say the Lancaster, all told.'

'Ring the bell, Everett.'

He did so, and a lively blonde, familiar with her forties but nicely preserved, bounced through from reception. Our eyes went shyly down. She took a glass to shine as she waited our call. Type of lass who needs her hands occupied.

'Do you for, gents?'

Irish, her accent.

'Round of the Lancaster, wasn't it?' said Everett.

She squinted towards our table, counted the heads.

'Times six,' confirmed Everett.

The landlady squinted harder. She dropped the glass. It smashed to pieces on the floor.

'Maurice?' she said.

It was Mo that froze, stared, softened.

'B-B-Barbara?' he said.

We watched as he rose and crossed to the bar. A man in a dream was Mo. We held our breaths as Mo and Barbara took each other's hands over the counter. They were wordless for some moments, and then felt ten eyes on them, for they giggled, and Barbara set blushing to the Lancasters. She must have spilled half again down the slops gully as she poured. I joined Everett to carry the ales to our table. Mo and Barbara went into a huddle down the far end of the counter. They were rapt.

Real Ale Club would not have marked Mo for a romancer.

'The quiet ones you watch,' said Tom N. 'Maurice?'

'Mo? With a piece?' whispered Everett Bell.

'Could be they're old family friends,' tried innocent Billy. 'Or relations?'

Barbara was now slowly stroking Mo's wrist.

'Four buggerin' fishwives I'm sat with,' said John Mosely. 'What are we to make of these Lancasters?'

We talked ale but were distracted. Our glances cut down the length of the bar. Mo and Barbara talked lowly, quickly, excitedly down there. She was moved by Mo, we could see that plain enough. Again and again she ran her fingers through her hair. Mo was gazing at her, all dreamy, and suddenly he'd got a thumb hooked in the belt-loop of his denims – Mr Suave. He didn't so much as touch his ale.

Next, of course, the jaunty landlord arrived back on the scene.

'Oh, Alvie!' she cried. 'You'll never guess!'

'Oh?' said the landlord, all the jauntiness instantly gone from him.

'This is *Maurice!*'

'Maurice?' he said. 'You're joking . . .'

It was polite handshakes then, and feigned interest in Mo on the landlord's part, and a wee fat hand he slipped around the small of his wife's back.

'We'll be suppin' up,' said John Mosely, sternly.

Mo had a last, whispered word with Barbara but her smile was fixed now and the landlord remained in close attendance. As we left, Mo looked back and raised his voice a note too loud. Desperate, he was.

'Barbara?'

We dragged him along. We'd had word of notable pork scratchings up the Mangy Otter.

'Do tell, Maur*ice*,' said Tom N.

'Leave him be,' said John Mosely.

'An ex, that's all,' said Mo.

And Llandudno was infernal. Families raged in the heat. All of the kids wept. The Otter was busyish when we sludged in. We settled on a round of St Austell Tributes from a meagre selection. Word had not been wrong on the quality of the scratchings. And the St Austell turned out to be in top form.

'I'd be thinking in terms of a seven,' said Everett Bell.

'Or a shade past that?' said John Mosely.

'You could be right on higher than sevens,' said Billy Stroud. 'But surely we're not calling it an eight?'

'Here we go,' I said.

'Now this,' said Billy Stroud, 'is where your 7.5s would come in.'

'We've heard this song, Billy,' said John Mosely.

'He may not be wrong, John,' said Everett.

'Give him a 7.5,' said John Mosely, 'and he'll be wanting his 6.3s, his 8.6s. There'd be no bloody end to it!'

'Tell you what,' said Mo. 'How about I catch up with you all a bit later? Where's next on the list?'

We stared at the carpet. It had diamonds on and crisps ground into it.

'Next up is the Crippled Ox on Burton Square,' I read from my printout. 'Then it's Henderson's on Old Parade.'

'See you at one or the other,' said Mo.

He threw back the dregs of his St Austell and was gone.

We decided on another at the Otter. There was a Whitstable Silver Star, 6.2 per cent to volume, a regular stingo to settle our nerves.

'What's the best you've ever had?' asked Tom N.

It's a conversation that comes up again and again but it was a life-saver just then: it took our minds off Mo.

'Put a gun to my head,' said Big John, 'and I don't think I could look past the draught Bass I had with me dad in Peter Kavanagh's. Sixteen years of age, Friday teatime, first wage slip in my arse pocket.'

'But was it the beer or the occasion, John?'

'How can you separate the two?' he said, and we all sighed.

'For depth? Legs? Back-note?' said Everett Bell. 'I'd do well to ever best the Swain's Anthem I downed a November Tuesday in Stockton-on-Tees: 19 and 87. 4.2 per cent to volume. I was still in haulage at that time.'

'I've had an Anthem,' said Billy Stroud of this famously hard-to-find brew, 'and I'd have to say I found it an unexceptional ale.'

Everett made a face.

'So what'd be your all-time, Billy?'

The ex-Marxist knitted his fingers atop the happy mound of his belly.

'Ridiculous question,' he said. 'There is so much wonderful ale on this island. How is a sane man to separate a Pelham High Anglican from a Warburton's Saxon Fiend? And we haven't even mentioned the great Belgian tradition. Your Duvel's hardly a dishwater. Then there's the Czechs, the Poles, the Germans . . .'

'Gassy pop!' cried Big John, no fan of a German brew, of a German anything.

'Nonsense,' said Billy. 'A Paulaner Weissbier is a sensational sup on its day.'

'Where'd you think Mo's headed?' Tom N cut in.

Everett groaned:

'He'll be away down the Prom View, won't he? Big ape.'

'Mo a ladykiller?' said Tom. 'There's one for breaking news.'

'No harm if it meant he smartened himself up a bit,' said John.

'He has let himself go,' said Billy. 'Since the testicle.'

'You'd plant spuds in those ears,' I said.

The Whitstables had us in fighting form. We were away up the Crippled Ox. We found there a Miner's Slattern on cask. TV news showed sardine beaches and motorway chaos. There was an internet machine on the wall, a pound for ten minutes, and Billy Stroud went to consult the meteorological satellites. The Slattern set me pensive

Strange, I thought, how I myself had wound up a Real Ale Club stalwart. 1995, October, I'd found myself in motorway services outside Ormskirk having a screaming barny with the missus. We were moving back to her folks' place in Northern Ireland. From dratted Leicester. We were heading for the ferry at Stranraer. At services, missus told me I was an idle lardarse who had made her life hell and she never wanted to see me again. We'd only stopped off to fill the tyres. She gets in, slams the door, puts her foot down. Give her ten minutes, I thought, she'll calm down and turn back for me. Two hours later, I'm sat in an empty Chinese in services, weeping, and eating Szechuan beef. I call a taxi. Taxi comes. I says where are we, exactly? Bloke looks at me. He says Ormskirk direction. I says what's the nearest city of any size? Drop you in Liverpool for twenty quid, he says. He leaves me off downtown and I look for a pub. Spot the Ship and Mitre and in I go. I find a stunning row of pumps. I call a Beaver Mild out of Devon.

'I wouldn't,' says a bloke with a beard down the bar.

'Oh?'

'Try a Marston's Old Familiar,' he says, and it turns out he's Billy Stroud.

The same Billy turned from the internet machine at the Ox in Llandudno.

'37.9,' he said. 'Bristol Airport, a shade after three. Flights delayed, tarmac melting.'

'Pig heat,' said Tom N.

'We won't suffer much longer,' said Billy. 'There's a change due.'

'Might get a night's sleep,' said Everett.

The hot nights were certainly a torment. Lying there with a sheet stuck to your belly. Thoughts coming loose, beer fumes rising, a manky arse. The city beyond the flat throbbing with summer. Usually I'd get up and have a cup of tea, watch some telly. Astrophysics on Beeb Two at four in the morning, news from the galaxies, and light already in the eastern sky. I'd dial the number in Northern Ireland and then hang up before they could answer.

Mo arrived into the Ox like the ghost of Banquo. There were terrible scratch marks down his left cheek.

'A Slattern will set you right, kid,' said John Mosely, discreetly, and he manoeuvred his big bones barwards.

Poor Mo was wordless as he stared into the ale that was put before him. Billy Stroud sneaked a time-out signal to Big John.

'We'd nearly give Henderson's a miss,' agreed John.

'As well get back to known terrain,' said Everett.

We climbed the hot streets towards the station. We stocked up with some Cumberland Pedigrees, 3.4 per cent to volume, always an easeful drop. The train was busy with daytrippers heading back. We sipped quietly. Mo looked half dead as he slumped there but now and then he'd come up for a mouthful of his Pedigree.

'How's it tasting, kiddo?' chanced Everett.

'Like a ten,' said Mo, and we all laughed.

The flicker of his old humour reassured us. The sun descended on Colwyn Bay and there was young life everywhere. I'd only spoken to her once since Ormskirk. We had details to finalise, and she was happy to let it slip about her new bloke. Some twat called Stan.

'He's emotionally spectacular,' she said.

'I'm sorry to hear it, love,' I said. 'Given you've been through the wringer with me.'

'I mean in a good way!' she barked. 'I mean in a *calm* way!'

We'd a bit of fun coming up the Dee Estuary with the Welsh place names.

'Fy . . . feen . . . no. Fiiiif . . . non . . . fyff . . . non . . . growy?'

This was Tom N.

'Foy. Nonn. Grewey?'

This was Everett's approximation.

'Ffynnongroew,' said Billy Stroud, lilting it perfectly. 'Simple. And this one coming up? Llannerch-y-mor.'

Pedigree came down my nose I laughed that hard.

'Young girl, beautiful,' said Mo. 'Turn around and she's forty bloody three.'

'Leave it, Mo,' said Big John.

But he could not.

'She's come over early in '86. She's living up top of the Central line, Theydon Bois. She's working in a pub there, live-in, and ringing me from a phone box. In Galway I'm in a phone box too – we have to arrange the times, eight o'clock on Tuesday, ten o'clock on Friday. It's physical fucking pain she's not in town any more. I'll follow in the summer is the plan and I get there, Victoria Coach Station, six in the morning, eighty quid in my pocket. And she's waiting for me there. We have an absolute dream of a month. We're lying in the park. There's a song out and we make it our song. "Oh to be in England, in the summertime, with my love, close to the edge".'

'Art of Noise,' said Billy Stroud.

'Shut up, Billy!'

'Of course the next thing the summer's over and I've a start with BT up here and she's to follow on, October is the plan. We're ringing from phone boxes again, Tuesdays and Fridays but the second Friday the phone doesn't ring. Next time I see her she's forty bloody three.'

Flint station we passed through, and then Connah's Quay.

'Built up, this,' said Tom N. 'There's an Aldi, look? And that's a new school, is it?'

'Which means you want to be keeping a good two hundred yards back,' said Big John.

We were horrified. Through a miscarriage of justice, plain as, Tom N had earlier in the year been placed on a sex register. Oh the world is mad! Tom N is a placid, placid man. We were all six of us quiet as the grave on the evening train then. It grew and built, it was horrible, the silence. It was Everett at last that broke it; we were coming in for Helsby. Fair dues to Everett.

'Not like you, John,' he said.

Big John nodded.

'I don't know where that came from, Tom,' he said. 'A bloody stupid thing to say.'

Tom N raised a palm in peace but there was no disguising the hurt that had gone in. I pulled away into myself. The turns the world takes – Tom dragged through the courts, Everett half mad, Mo all scratched up and one-balled, Big John jobless for eighteen months. Billy Stroud was content, I suppose, in Billy's own way. And there was me, shipwrecked in Liverpool. Funny, for a while, to see 'Penny Lane' flagged up on the buses, but it wears off.

And then it was before us in a haze. Terrace rows we passed, out Speke way, with cookouts on the patios. Tiny pockets of glassy laughter we heard through the open windows of the carriage. Families and what-have-you. We had the black hole of the night before us – it wanted filling. My grimmest duty as publications officer was the obits page of the newsletter. Too many had passed on at forty-four, at forty-six.

'I'm off outings,' I announced. 'And I'm off bloody publications as well.'

'You did volunteer on both counts,' reminded Big John.

'It would leave us in an unfortunate position,' said Tom N.

'For my money, it's been a very pleasant outing,' said Billy Stroud.

'We've supped some quality ale,' concurred Big John.

'We've had some cracking weather,' said Tom N.

'Llandudno is quite nice, really,' said Mo.

Around his scratch marks an angry bruising had seeped. We all looked at him with tremendous fondness.

''Tis nice,' said Everett Bell. 'If you don't run into a she-wolf.'

'If you haven't gone ten rounds with Edward bloody Scissorhands,' said John Mosely.

We came along the shabby grandeurs of the city. The look on Mo's face then couldn't be read as anything but happiness.

'Maurice,' teased Big John, 'is thinking of the rather interesting day he's had.'

Mo shook his head.

'Thinking of days I had years back,' he said.

It has this effect, Liverpool. You're not back in the place five minutes and you go sentimental as a famine ship. We piled off at Lime Street. There we go: six big blokes in the evening sun.

'There's the Lion Tavern?' suggested Tom N.

'There's always the Lion,' I agreed.

'They've a couple of Manx ales guesting at Rigby's,' said Everett Bell.

'Let's hope they're an improvement on previous Manx efforts,' said Billy Stroud.

'There's the Grapes?' tried Big John.

'There's always the Grapes,' I agreed.

And alewards we went about the familiar streets. The town was in carnival: Tropic of Lancashire in a July swelter. It would not last. There was rain due in off the Irish Sea, and not for the first time.

ERNESTINE AND KIT

Two ladies in their sixties made ground through north County Sligo in a neat Japanese car. The sky above Lough Gill was deep blue and the world was fat on the blood of summer. The speed limit was carefully abided and all the turns were slowed for. There was the carnival air of a fine Saturday in June. A vintage car show had drawn a crowd in 1920s boaters and blazers to Kilmore; the old Fords and Triumphs honked cheerfully in the sun, and the ladies as they passed by smiled and waved. There was a lengthy queue for the ferry ride to the lake isle of Inishfree, there were castles to be visited, and way-marked walks to be hotly trailed. All the shaded tables outside the village pubs were full and tinkled with glasses and laughter, and children played unguarded in the cool of the woods.

'When it gets a good old lick of weather at all,' Ernestine said, 'this is one powerful country.'

'No place to compare,' Kit sighed, and the summer growth swished heavily against the Toyota's side windows on a tight bend after Tully.

Ernestine was big, with the high colour of a carnivore, and her haunches strained a little against the capacity of her cream linen trousers in the confined space of the driver's seat. Her mottled, fleshy arms were held tensely erect as she steered – she had learned to drive later in life. Kit, slightly the younger, was long-necked, tightly permed, and thin as a cable. She had a darting glance that scanned the country they passed through and by habit she drew her companion's attention to places and people of interest.

'Would they be hair extensions?' she wondered, as they passed a young blonde pushing a pram along the roadside verge.

'You can bet on it,' Ernestine said. 'The way they're streaked with that silvery-looking, kind of . . .'

'Cheap-looking,' Kit said.

'Yes.'

'Gaudy!'

'A young mother,' Ernestine said.

'Got up like a tuppenny whore,' Kit said.

'The skirt's barely down past her modesty, are you watching?'

'I am watching. And that horrible, *horrible* stonewash denim!'

'Where would the whore be headed for, Kit?'

Kit consulted the road map.

'Leckaun is the next place along,' she said. 'Only a stretch up the road from here. Her ladyship is headed into a pub, no doubt.'

'Drinking cider with fellas with earrings and tattoos,' Ernestine said. 'In by a pool table. In a dank old back room. Dank!'

'You can only imagine,' said Kit, and she made the sign of the cross. 'A jukebox and beer barrels and cocaine in the toilets. The misfortunate infant left to its own devices.'

'Would we nearly stall for a while in Leckaun, Kit?'

Kit pondered this a moment.

'No,' she decided, 'we'll hit on for the castle. There'll be a nice crowd there for sure.'

Onwards through the county the Toyota mildly sped, and the ladies had the windows buzzed down a little for breeze: it brought the medieval scent of the old-growth woods. They had been on the road since early morning but there was no tiredness yet – the excitement of the outing countered that.

'A Cornetto would go down a treat,' Ernestine said.

'Ice-cream weather most certainly,' Kit replied.

They turned to smile at each other. They hoped to have the need to buy ice creams soon enough, and more than two.

Castles were good. The car park was almost entirely full. Ernestine manoeuvred – after a couple of chubby attempts that brought sweat to her forehead – into the last available space. As the engine cut the car filled with the sound of anxious birds and the nearby chatter of the castle visitors. For a moment, the ladies pleasantly listened – they did love a summer-afternoon crowd. The lake waters the castle kept guard of sat as heavily as the blue sky above; each was a suspension of the other.

'Or would we chance a scone, Kit?'

'It would hardly put us in the ground, Ernestine.'

The coffee shop, housed in a sensitive glass extension to the castle, was beautifully busy. Bored dads and tired mams lolled there over gazpacho soup and expensive sandwiches – there was organic cola and baked treats for the kiddies. Ernestine and Kit took their places in the thick of it all. Often, in the quiet winter months, back in the bungalow, in the midlands, they spoke of how it was they were perceived in the world. What were they taken for, they wondered, out there amid the light and gatherings of summer? Maiden aunts, they supposed, or a pair of nuns who had left – after some shabby soul-wrenching – their order, or maybe as discreet lesbians just a little too aged for openness. What was certain was they would be taken for gentle, kind souls with their aunt-like smiles to seal the contrivance.

They nibbled hungrily as mice at the buttered fruit scones. The tea was left to brew until it was strong as ale. It was poured with satisfaction. They watched carefully the crowd at the cafeteria. They spoke icily of the little darlings who everywhere wobbled between the legs of tables and stumbled over shoulder bags left thoughtlessly on the floor – people just didn't think as to what might trip a child. The scones were about done with when Kit gobbled nervously along the length of her slender neck, and she reached a hand for Ernestine's.

'Look!'

Kit nodded sharply. It was a single hard gesture aimed at a little girl, almost albino-pale. She wore sky-blue shorts of a thin fleece material, silver-buckled sandals patterned with daisies, and a striped, armless French top.

'Oh, an angel, Kit!'

'Hush!'

'Oh, perfection.'

The girl was part of a family of four. The mother was as pale and fair-haired, a weary prettiness persisting into her late thirties. There was a brother, perhaps twice the girl's age, hunched over a hand-held video game – they heard at fifteen yards its *bleeps* and *kapows*. The father was sallow and dark-haired.

'Daddy's a greasy-looking Herbert,' Ernestine said.

'Would he be foreign?'

'Is the child nearly his at all, you'd wonder?'

'If 'tis, his blood is weak.'

'Might have a manner of a . . . Portuguese, have we?'

'And as sour-looking as it's greasy.'

Quiet outrage bubbled in their insides. Oh, the undeserving bastards who were blessed with the presence of angels.

'The mother is a liar,' Kit said.

'Would you read her so, Kit?'

'I would. She has a liar's chin.'

They waited at distance for the family to finish up. They prayed that they had encountered them at the right time, that they were at the start and not the finish of their visit. They were rewarded when the family rose from the table and aimed not for the car park but for the castle's interior. The family went dutifully through the cool hallways, and Ernestine and Kit followed; carefully, they drifted into the melt of visitors, there by the chain mail and the crests of arms and the dark stonewalls.

The parents were not careful with the little girl. She roamed ten and twelve and fifteen feet away from them. And that could be enough, in the labyrinth of a castle, a place of quick turns and sudden twists, and the child was forgotten for a half-minute at a time, and that too could be enough.

Ernestine felt a slow hot flush creep her shoulders and ascend her neck.

Kit tinily in the dry pit of her throat made a cage bird's excited trilling.

The albino sheen of the child's hair was a perfect tracer in the crowd.

'Are you looking at the backs of her knees?' Ernestine whispered.

'How so?'

'I mean the little folds of flesh there, look? There's still pup fat on her!'

'Ah there is. Ah sweetness!'

The family as it moved with the afternoon crowd broke down into a spat. The father shouted at the little boy, who was showing great interest in his video game but none at all in Ireland's heritage. The lazy blur of the crowd's movement was watched closely by Kit for the blocking it would afford; Ernestine's eyes were locked on the girl child. The mother scolded the father for his shouting – an index finger was wielded at his face. The father seethed and snapped a remark. The boy was in the zone only of his game. The tiny girl was for a moment forgotten.

'Move,' Kit said.

Ernestine slipped a tube of wine gums from her bag and as she moved her smile was warmed by her desire to have the child's heat – if briefly – in her life.

'I think I know your name, sweetie thing?'

The girl was perhaps twenty feet from her parents at this carefully chosen moment – it was as good as a mile – and she repaid Ernestine's fuzzy smile at once with a gap-toothed grin of her own.

'My name?'

The mother and father argued yet, their backs still turned, and the boy still lost to his hand-held world.

'Oh I know your name for certain, I'd say! Would I have a little guess at it?'

The child giggled.

'I'd say your name could be written on one of these . . .'

She showed the sweets and popped one loose.

'Yes, yes,' she was beside the girl now, and she leaned in confidingly, and she squinted hard at the wine gum in her hand, as if a name was inscribed there. 'It says here that you're a . . . Bob?'

The child laughed, and tossed her head to show the crooked milk teeth, and the white filmy ooze of babyhood that coated still her gums, and she flicked coquettishly her hair – she was surely no Bob – and, unseen, Kit circled and moved in behind her, paused for a check, and then moved closer.

You might travel the length of Ireland for weeks on end, down all the great yawning of the summer days, and you would never come across the ideal moment. But sometimes the luck came in.

'Can't be! Oh, it can't be a Bob! Maybe you're someone else altogether. Maybe I need to have a closer look now, my darling, and we'll find out what your name is yet.'

Ernestine's fingers trailed the filigree down of the child's bare arm. The slightest of touches was electric, and enough to distract her – her eyes became bloodshot – and Ernestine withdrew from it carefully. She shucked another wine gum free and examined it intently.

'Now it says here, we have a . . . is it a Kathy? An Aoife? Is it a Megan? Is it . . .'

She turned her head close to the child.

'Allie,' the child said.

'Oh baby Allie,' Ernestine said, and a tear came and ran slowly her cheek.

She gave the girl the wine gum. Allie chewed on it. And

Ernestine moved in and tickled her beneath the arm, and whisperingly she sang:

'Allie's so pretty, Allie's so sweet, Allie is the little girl who's walkin' down your street . . .'

She raised her head and blinked her eyes rapidly then for her companion.

'Take her, Kit!'

At precisely this moment, as Kit took the little girl warmly inside a cuddle that was also a lock, with her skinny forearm placed just so over the child's mouth; as she lifted Allie high and close to her; as Ernestine rose and pressed Kit on the small of the back, and hissed –

'Go! Go!'

– it was at this moment that Allie's brother drew her into the row. He gestured in her direction – he knew his sister's whereabouts by instinct – and he squealed at his parents that Allie was allowed to do as she pleased, that she was never forced to . . .

As he spoke, the family all turned and they saw her, in the distance, in the arms of the lady with the tight perm.

'Allie!'

The mother's desperate scream was signal enough for Kit to pinch viciously the pup fat at the back of Allie's knees, causing the child to shriek and cry. The pinch was Kit's procedure in such an emergency: upset in the child would justify the ladies' intrusion.

'Oh hush, baby, hush! Oh look it, look it . . . is this your mammy now . . . is this mammykins?'

The mother fell drunkenly on her child, and Ernestine took the father's forearm.

'Oh thank God!' she said. 'She was so upset! We were

going for security! She thought she had ye lost altogether.'

'Oh thank you so much,' said the father.

'Oh Allie, honey, shush!' cried the mother.

'Is that her name, is it Allie, isn't she some beauty?'

'Allie, we were only over there! Sweetheart, what is it?'

'Ah she couldn't see ye and the poor thing get herself all fussed.'

'Ah poor baby Allie.'

In a chorus of cooings the matter was smoothed over, and Ernestine and Kit were gratefully thanked for coming to the aid of a small child in distress. The family was left intact, with Allie still weeping, and the ladies moved on with fond smiles and waves. They turned at once for the car park. They made it only just in time. As the Toyota moved, the father dashed into the sightline of the rearview mirror – the angel had spoken – but he was too late, and if he got the reg it was no matter. The plates were false, having been fixed that morning in the garage attached to the bungalow.

They sped twenty and thirty and forty kilometres beyond the speed limit through Sligo and into Leitrim and then Cavan. It was a useful tactic then to drive into Northern Ireland, a separate jurisdiction – the ladies planned for failure as much as success, failure being the commonplace – and it was not until they had crossed the bridge that marks the border, where Blacklion gives way to Belcoo, that they permitted themselves speech again.

'I'll tell you this much,' Ernestine said. 'I would not like to see a read of my blood pressure right now.'

'It'd be crazy,' Kit scolded.

They drove on, and at length they settled to the miserable fact that the day was done for.

'As we're on the road,' Kit said, 'we could hit the Asda in Enniskillen and pick up some wine.'

The cheaper wines from north of the border would provide a small consolation when they returned, just the two of them, to the floral-patterned walls of the bungalow. It lay blamelessly behind a windbreak of pines – the trees created about the home an aura of great silence. Birds did not nest in those trees ever.

Quickly, the Toyota was on the outskirts of Enniskillen, and traffic was heavy. Another festival – this time by the Erne – drew crowds to its merries, and the air was thick with barbecue smoke that travelled over the water. The afternoon ascended to its peak; the heat was terrific. They saw a shaven-headed, shirtless man and his long, dark-haired partner as they walked towards the carnival, with a small child between them, a little boy.

'Are you watching,' Ernestine said, 'the creature with the head?'

'Would have the look of a soldier,' Kit said. 'A squaddie.'

The Toyota stalled at traffic lights and the family passed directly in front. The ladies regarded each other dolefully.

'A fine environment for a child,' Ernestine said. 'To be growing up in a house where the father has a pierced nipple.'

'The look of drink off him as well.'

'Oh it's sweating out of his every pore, Kit!'

In truth, they weren't shy themselves with the New Zealand Cabernet Sauvignon, four pounds sterling the screwtop bottle. They went through it by the crate, with the radio set to Lyric FM, the classical station, and it played late, always, into the bungalow's night, with Ernestine leafing through her power-tool catalogues, and Kit with her small-hours glaze on, and her occasional trilling.

They went sulkily about the aisles of Asda. They filled a trolley with the wine. They bought frozen mince in five-kilo packages. They bought kitchen towel in the fattest available rolls – they went through such an amount of it. Tiredness caught up and it carried age's taste. The migraine glare of the aisle lights was a trial, and so too was the drone and chill of the refrigeration, and so too the futile cheeps of the piped music. The day was marked by and was heavy with failure, and it was as if their luck might never change but as they neared, by fate, the customer services desk, it did. An announcement was made: a toddler had been found, and its parents should approach at once – the child was panicked.

Boldly, the chance was taken.

'Oh my darling Allie!'

Ernestine at a dash reached the desk, and she flung herself on the child, and Kit was at her back, and she kept watch; she knew they had perhaps a minute, maximum, no matter how vast the Asda.

'Oh thank you so much!' Kit cried. 'Oh thank you.'

'Ah she's upset, she got a wee shock, a wee shock is all . . .' Ernestine soothed as the toddler continued to scream.

The customer services lady was delighted to have reunited the odd family – 'Allie, is that her name?' she said. 'Pretty.' Delighted to be rid of the screaming child, she waved them along.

Held in a firm lock by Kit's steel-wire arms, it was a monstrously burbling infant they carried at pace across the car park – their trolley abandoned to the air-conditioned aisle. Quickly they were away, and Ernestine through the busy town gunned the Toyota.

Belcoo.

Blacklion.

Dromahair.

And now they began their descent to the midland plain, and the toddler wailed itself to a state of purple exhaustion, and it was laid on the back seat.

Kit after a time turned and eyed it coldly.

'This is no angel,' she said.

Ernestine consulted the rearview and tightened her lips in agreement.

'Is it not kind of . . . wall-eyed, Kit?'

'It is. And a jaundicey class of a look to it, I'd say. Once the purple clears.'

On a straight stretch, Ernestine turned to give the child a more considered appraisal.

'I wouldn't think we'll be depriving the world of an Einstein,' she said.

'No indeed.'

'Bad blood, Kit.'

'Sure what kind of parents? Can you imagine, Ernie? What kind of parents would lose a child in an Asda?'

'Drunks and drug addicts and prostitutes,' Ernestine said.

'With tattoos on their backsides,' Kit said.

'It smells, Kit.'

'Oh, a smell that would knock you, Ernestine.'

'Look at the Babygro!'

'It's busting out of it.'

'Fattish alright. Being fed on white bread mulched down with milk and cane sugar.'

'Asda-bought the Babygro.'

'Oh, classy.'

'Could it be . . .'

'What, Kit?'

'Could it be an itinerant we have on our hands?'

'Oh Jesus Christ, a tinker child!'

'Ernestine, what I'd say to you now . . .'

'I know, darling.'

'Do you?'

'You're right, darling.'

'I am! The likes of this . . . *thing* isn't worth the effort nor the risk.'

The decision was made. The Toyota pulled into a lay-by. The toddler was lifted by Kit from the back seat. It was taken across a ditch and left beneath hawthorn bushes – a kindness to give it shade from the sun that was hot still. The Toyota with relief departed the lay-by, and headed for home, the bungalow, the windbreak pines planted in the soft give of an earth that hid so efficiently.

Near the lay-by as the evening aged the toddler sat silently beneath the hawthorn; it was stunned. It blinked against the midges that came up from the lake to feast on it but it had no strength left to cry. With interest, the toddler was watched by a pair of hooded crows, who stalked about importantly – like fascist birds, like jackboot gestapo – who waited on its final weakening, and for its sore eyes to sleepily close.

THE MAINLAND CAMPAIGN

Camden High Street, Sunday morning, 11 a.m.

He stood with Manus by the elevator in the tube station as the crowds rose up in a great surge of bodies and voices.

'It's a scrum of people alright,' Manus said.

'Wait till you see it coming on for one o'clock,' he said. 'Once the hungover fuckers have woken up.'

Sunday morning meant Camden Market and all the tribes were headed for it: the goths and the punks, the rockabillies, the acid-house kids.

'You're one twisted fucker, Steven. Did I ever tell you that?'

'The way it works,' he said, 'is there's a kind of honour thing with the buskers.'

An old hippy slapped his guitar and wailed a Neil Young song by the base of the elevator.

'They take it in turns,' he said. 'When you leave your guitar case down beside the fella singing, it means you're next in line. You go off and have a cup of tea and a smoke.'

'Jesus Christ.'

'That's it. Sundays, you get a half-hour each by the moving stair. Is the arrangement.'

'The fucking crowd,' Manus said.

'It's nothing yet,' Steven said proudly. 'One o'clock? You can't breathe for people coming up that stair.'

They were a dozen to the cell. They came from north Tipperary, south Limerick, north Kerry. Steven was the one they had chosen. The young fella was lethal. They could tell that by the set of mouth on him. Also he had the blood.

'This day week?' Steven said.

'I can try,' Manus said. 'A fucking guitar case.'

They went into the hot morning sun. Even the pure unmoving heat of July was a relief after the crush of the tube station. They headed down the High Street among the crowds.

'Some collection of fucking poofters,' Manus said.

The goths sold bootleg tapes from briefcases stacked on bakers' pallets: Sisters of Mercy live in Amsterdam. The punks sat on the ground on the corner of Inverness Street and drank cider with their dogs. The rockabillies headed for the early dance show at Camden Lock. The acid-house kids bounced about like rubber toys and beamed madly as they headed into the warren of the market stalls. There were two blokes in old-fashioned gowns outside the Electric Ballroom.

'Some collection of homos,' Manus said.

They went along past the veg stalls of Inverness Street. A graffito on the wall read:

'88 Summer Of Love – Enjoy This Trip

They went into the Good Mixer which had no more than a scatter of old men at its tables yet. Manus bought the two pints and they played a game of pool.

'How you fixed anyway?'

'I'm not so bad,' Steven said.

'You at the French restaurant yet?'

'Kensington Church Street.'

'You're turning out the gourmet cuisine for 'em, you are?'

'I'm KP,' Steven said. 'Kitchen porter.'

'Nice way of putting it for a pot scrubber.'

'Well.'

'Charles and Di down that way, no?'

'Not far.'

'You'd have an aul' lick off her and all, wouldn't you?'

Manus was a dog man from north Kerry. There wasn't much wrong with the back end of a greyhound he couldn't fix. He worked often at the Walthamstow track. He was the only one that Steven met with on a regular basis. That was the best practice, no question. Everybody studied the practice. Late at night, in the farmhouses and semi-ds – the practice.

Steven named bottom left for the black and made the shot easily.

'Handy,' Manus said.

Steven was seventeen the month of June gone. He had a black mass of backcombed hair and a graveyard pallor. His uniform daily was motorcycle boots and black army trousers, no matter the weather. He lived in a squat near Goodge Street station. The building was owned by Arabs and the apartments were for short-term lets. There were always at least half of them empty. Change the locks and they had to give you six months' notice to get out.

'What'll you do after?'

'I'll go to a pub and watch the news,' Steven said.

'Wear your eyeliner,' Manus said. 'Keep the hair up. Wear all the gear, yeah?'

'No fear,' Steven said.

Polly, the restaurant manager, was most attractive when she was angry with him.

'The telephone,' she said, 'is for bookings only. It's not for your personal use, Steven. It's not for casual calls.'

She talked to him as if he wasn't exactly in the same place as her. He'd been called up from the basement kitchen to the phone in the restaurant. It was not good for business – the sight of Steven with the sauce stains and the hair and the boots.

'It wasn't casual. It was important.'

'Never again.'

It had been Manus on the phone. The guitar was fixed and ready for Sunday. Polly clipped away on her heels, and he was left to the KP corner – it was a mess of steam from the washer and towers of stacked plates and ancient sinks stained with green and brownish moulds. The way it was in the kitchen, if nobody was looking, he'd fork a couple of baby new potatoes somebody had left on their side dish and run them through the creamy sauce in the bain-marie. Nigel, the chef, caught him at the caper with the potatoes one day.

'Pat likes his spuds,' he said.

The shift was ten until three, six days a week, and the money was dirt but it filled the hours as he waited. Walking to the tube after, he enjoyed the warm air of the street, and he bought a tin of lager in the Paki shop – his new routine – and he sipped it as he went. He played tapes on the Walkman, his own compilations. They had been made in the bedroom at home before he had travelled. He hopped the barrier at the station – he had not so far bought a ticket.

Back in the squat, he lay on the mattress and he halfways slept and he had an erection. The excitement of the night lay ahead, and it was a great distraction from the Sunday.

It was 'Feet First' at the Camden Palace on Thursdays. He showered for it even. He had not yet managed to hook up the electric for the squat and the shower was ice-cold and reviving. He burned a candle in the windowless bathroom for the mirror and he got himself made up to the hilt. He drank from a bottle of red wine as he worked on his face. He set water to boil on the Argos campstove he had bought with his first wages. When the water was ready, he stirred five spoons of sugar into it, and with careful fingers he worked the mixture into his hair, teasing out the strands until they were high and as if wind-blown.

All summer long he had been in rut heat and lonesome. He was in love with the girl in the Italian chipper. He was in love with Polly the restaurant manager. He was in love with the middle-aged lady who pulled pints at Presley's and called him 'Ducky'.

'You'll have your Guinness, Ducky?'

He was in love with every girl on the Northern line as it aimed for Camden. The anticipation built, and as he entered the Palace he trembled. At 'Feet First' they played everything he wanted to hear – unbelievable, it might have been his own collection he was listening to. Sisters of Mercy, The Mission, Einstürzende Neubauten, one after the other, all night long.

He saw her dance nearby. She was a blonde girl, not English he could tell, and the blonde looked good against the black of her clothes.

'Sab . . .'

'Ina.'

'S.A.B.I.N.A?'

'Yes.'

She worked for a doctor in the Black Forest. She was a housekeeper there. She was in the city for two weeks only. She was staying with her aunt. He kissed her and she took to it and they kissed and felt each other for a long time then on the dark seats by the sideways. He could see a village in the German woods with great trees all about. He could feel the cool and fresh air. Her English was not advanced but they could talk well enough and it felt easy to be with Sabina. After the music had ended, they sat on the railings on Camden High Street for a while and talked and kissed more.

'You around tomorrow at all?'

'I have to go with my friend.'

'You around Saturday?'

'I go to Brighton with my aunt.'

'Ah yeah.'

'But maybe on Sunday?'

'Sunday?'

'I will be at the market?'

She told him of the motorcycle boots she planned to buy at Camden Market on the Sunday. He said he knew the exact stall. He asked what time did she expect to be around and she said maybe lunchtime. If he liked, she would meet him there. Half-past twelve was the time they agreed. Outside the station.

He walked her back to her aunt's flat on Kentish Town Road. He talked about the difference between being in Ireland and being in England, as he saw it.

'Ireland is magical,' he said. 'England is ironical.'

He liked the sound of that and she seemed to like it too. He kissed her once more in the doorway of the flatblock and it was a great hot and passionate kiss. He walked the long road home and was lit with desire for her. She was three years the older and this was very exciting. It was the first time he had kissed a woman in her twenties and everything in her kiss told him there could be more.

He could see himself living in a village in the Black Forest – it would take only a quick swerve and he was there. For some reason, he kept seeing an old-fashioned motorbike with a sidecar and Sabina sat in it, and the two of them in their boots. Twisting around the forest roads and slowing for the bends. Heading off somewhere for a feed of sausages and beer. To an inn.

He could not sleep that night for the heat in the squat. The excitements of the summer were almost too much to think about. So he did not think but listened only. He listened as the night slowly passed and there was half-light in the window by five and the rumble of the trains began again beneath the skin of the city. He listened as the traffic built. The early clankings and burr of the morning. It was daylight at last that poured a light sleep over him.

A housing estate in Tipperary, two winters previously.

He could hear the slow creaking and the catches of breath. He knew his mother had been fucking the nordy for the last week at least. He plugged his headphones into the stereo and turned the volume loud. The more they tried to muffle the noise, the more the images of their fucking projected.

He sat on the bed, cross-legged, stretching the cord of the headphones to its full extent. The nordy had been kept in the house since just after New Year.

Steven had the lights off. He twitched the curtains to look outside. A hard clear night with stars hung low on the estate. The estate was close in all around.

Now and then, a man would come and stay a while. The men were nordys often. His mother was from the north herself – she had moved down when it went bad. She had Steven a year after the move. She had him for an English fitter she met at a disco in Limerick. The fitter had stayed around for a few years only and he was just quick strokes of memory for Steven – the bristles of a beard, the softness of a wool shirt, the smell of his fags; the smell of the fags in the wool of the shirt. The men who came now were preceded always by a visit from Manus.

Steven was not allowed to speak with Manus – that was his mother's ruling.

The nordy slept in the boxroom. He watched the portable television in the small sitting room with the curtains drawn. He had his meals in the kitchen. He took some air in the yard out back if the days were dry and warm enough. Steven was not to speak with the nordy either but his mother was at work in the daytime and he did so. The nordy was quiet and made no fuss of anything. They would watch *Countdown* together. Steven went to the library for him. The nordy had requests – anything Elmore Leonard, anything John D. MacDonald.

One day Manus had called in daytime to see the nordy. Steven led him quietly through the house.

'That's some pair of boots,' Manus said. 'Size you take?'

'Twelves.'

'Fuck me. And what age are you now?'

Steven took off the headphones and looked outside to the estate; the slow nights of a winter. Their noise had ended and he pictured them resting. If he stayed awake long enough he knew he would hear the fucking start up again.

Tottenham Court Road, Sunday morning, 11 a.m.

The greatest insult was to call it the mainland campaign. If they were the mainland, we were what? He carried the guitar case as he walked. It was light as air.

'Slap it off a wall,' Manus had said, 'and it'll make no differ. She'll go when she's to go, hey?'

One o'clock was the time that was set. The morning was hot and dusty. He had slept soundly. There was the feeling of Sunday as he walked north for Camden. As he moved he felt the strength of his intention harden. Trash from the Saturday night went by in drifts of strange breeze about his feet.

He saw the dead bodies rise from their beds all over London. He saw them pull on red satin socks and brothel creepers with a leopardskin finish and scoop a palmful of Brylcreem through their hair. He saw nose rings clipped, and then the tartan trousers, and then the torn leather jacket. He saw faces he knew from 'Feet First', pale faces as gaunt even as Wayne from The Mission, and they too would be among the dead.

'The one thing you can't be is fucking emotional,' Manus had said. 'They say the "mainland" meaning the rest of the UK as opposed to the province of Ulster. They're not referring to the Republic at all. They're not saying the Republic isn't a mainland.'

'As if we don't exist even.'

'That's more of it you buck-fucking eejit! That's more of the emotional! If you're emotional how are you going to think straight? You've to stay clear in the head, Steven. Don't mind the fucking emotional.'

They saved what money they could from shit jobs and giros and kept it for the market on Sunday. They left squats and bedsits and made for the stations. From Tufnell Park, Brixton, Leytonstone. They were his own kind and if that was not proof of cold valour, what was?

He was on Camden High Street before he was aware of it. He went to the greasy spoon near the Good Mixer and he ordered a fried egg sandwich and a cup of tea. Two bites of the sandwich and he was on Inverness Street puking. He was annoyed at himself for that but there was no problem. He just had the look of another hungover scut on a Sunday morning.

There were slow hard minutes to be killed. He walked the backway to Camden Lock. He sat a while by the noodle stalls. He kept the case at his feet. He looked down at his boots. It came past noon.

He moved.

He felt steered as he walked along the High Street for the station. He passed by the Electric Ballroom. He saw the dead bodies climb out from the trains. The noise of Sunday on the High Street: the cockney boys selling lookalike threads – 'Armani Armani! Versace Versace!' – and the Sisters of Mercy blaring from ghetto blasters on the bakers' pallets and the gangsters in cars playing acid house and hip hop.

From the tube station the roar of the ascending crowd.

He'd leave the case that was set for one o'clock. He'd meet her outside at half twelve on the dot – surely a German would be on time. They could be in Regent's Park by the time it went, with her new boots bought. He waited outside a moment by the railings, Kentish Town Road side. He looked hard into the station. A response unit of the Met appeared in a sudden mob by the top of the elevator. There were a half-dozen of them, in riotwear, and a young goth was like a trapped animal between them, his arms all twisted.

The crowd splintered madly as the word went around:

'Bomb.'

'Bomb!'

'Bomb!'

The goth was pinned to the ground. Crowds broke onto the street in a panic – the station was cordoned. He picked up on the talk as he went with the crowd along the High Street. A guitar case the goth kid had carried was isolated for bomb disposal.

Manus.

That he was a match for the profile in the giddiness went unnoticed. He walked the length of the High Street again. He went along the canal, west, until he found a quiet spot beneath a bridge there. He hung the case over the rail but he could not let go of it. A wino sprawled on the far side of the canal called to him in an Irish accent:

'They're a hoor to learn, the guitars.'

He went back the pathway and he found an unseen moment among the Sunday crowd and he sneaked the case behind a bookstall on the Lock.

He was only ten minutes late for their meeting and she

looked as good in daylight. Camden was giving him a head-ache, he said, would they not get on a bus? She laughed, and she was taken with him, he could see that. They went to Hampstead to the repertory cinema there. They waited in the coffee shop for *Wings of Desire* to be screened. Other young people in black waited also.

'Ah yeah,' he said. 'Wim Wenders.'

'Vim,' she said.

'Hah?'

'You say it Vim Venders.'

'Right so.'

They watched angels over Berlin and he was transfixed. Afterwards, they walked, and he asked were there squats in Berlin? She said yes, there were many.

WISTFUL ENGLAND

He saw her every day as she moved through Stratford station. She came towards him on the concourse and the illusion held for just a moment. But as she came closer again her features would erase and re-form into someone else's – a stranger's. Still, he would search for her among the crush, each morning and evening, though she lived in another country, and he was not even romantic by nature.

His work involved threading fibre optic cables through office buildings. He tried not to stare too hard at the office girls, for she was among them, too – there were many who were slender and dark in that way. His heart was broken by them as he passed through the photocopier rooms. Most days he was rational, but he worried about the depth of his obsession, and he wondered, distantly, if it might turn to something darker.

Leytonstone had the air of just the kind of place a dark turn might occur. He shared a house off the High Road there with three peaceful alcoholics. He would drink with them for as long as he was able to at night and then pass out to dream the jagged, scratchy dreams that left him gaunt in the mornings. To be gaunt at twenty-five was a sombre accomplishment. He was putting money away but had no purpose in mind for it – he would not go back to Ireland. The weekends were the hardest.

He walked the evil local park on Saturday afternoon. The dads coddled their pitbulls and kicked balls at shaven-headed children. The light was giving up by four. He kept his eyes down as he passed the haggard masturbators who patrolled the territory of the public toilets. It was his usual bad luck that when the bell-ringer appeared to signal the park's closing, he did so directly behind him on the pathway, and he marched there, solemnly tolling, a harbinger, and each time he looked over his shoulder, on every third or fourth peel, the ringer was staring directly into him: a soul-reader in a parks jacket. He let himself be steered out of the park on the tip of the bell's ringing and he walked the High Road, where people at bus stops ate kebab meat and chips and the traffic looked as if it might do away with itself at any minute. January, and he turned down the long street of pre-war terrace houses on which he made his home. 'Humps for Half a Mile' a road sign read, warning of the traffic-calming measures that were in place, but the words had a metaphorical resonance. The house that he lived in was not a house in which he might casually talk of metaphors. It was not yet five o'clock but already his housemates had for some hours been going at the Excelsior lager. They were Connemara men, with the look of bunched and tragic navvies, though all three of them worked in IT. The Excelsior lager was 9.8 per cent to volume and would take the paint off the walls if left to its own devices. He settled into his usual armchair and received the usual vague smiles in greeting. They were watching gazelles in the forest wild – some dappled idyll in equatorial light

– but kept flicking back and forth to the BBC for the final
scores in the football.

'Fucken Lampard's on fire.'

'He fucken is the cunt.'

This was not a house in which to talk about the heart.
This was a house in which to drink super-strength lager and
cut yourself shaving. The bathroom in the mornings was
out of *Scarface*. He was not a fastidious man – he was
twenty-five – but the blood on the white tiles and the tiny
scraps of scrunched-up bloody toilet paper, these were hard
to stomach. His stomach was not the greatest anyway. He
had not been eating well for the best part of the year since
she had left him. Occasionally, a communal stew or casserole
was attempted in the house, but most often it was forgotten
about, causing smoke damage and small fires – the brigade
had been out more than once to number 126.

He could not keep the Excelsior down and always instead
drank Heineken. The housemates shook their heads at this
and accused him of gayness. But they were not lads overly
bothered by sex in any of its varieties. The Excelsior ruled
out attempts at courting and copulation. It pretty much
ruled out walking, too, and when more weed was required
from the Jamaican in the flats, he was, as always, the one
sent to fetch it. Soiled fivers were found in the pits of denims
and slapped into his hand; an ounce was agreed on for the
house to share. He drained what was left of his Heineken
and he stood up and into his jacket and he watched the last
few moments of the programme about gazelles.

'I thought they were going to be seen ridin' one another?'

'Hardly at this hour. Sure there's the watershed.'

The Jamaican's name was Rainbow and his lips were blue

from the crack pipe as he answered the door. The flat was kept as a shebeen and got out roughly as a kind of shanty-town bar. The curtains were tightly drawn and there were green fairy lights strung and there were bales of straw for decor and a lady somewhere in her thirties sat at a table licking the papers to seal a spliff. He followed Rainbow through the bar area to the kitchen and bought from him the ounce. Rainbow was not in the best of moods and called him a 'bloodclat' for no reason. Rainbow was unpredictable. To ease passage and smooth things out – he was a born diplomat – he bought a can of Red Stripe lager, also, and he went and sat with it at the table, by the lady, and they exchanged a smile, and she admitted handsomely that she was Rainbow's sister.

'A pleasure,' he said.

Rainbow played a ragga step-out on the sound system and could be heard back there to gurgle and hiss and his sister called to him to keep it down, would you, boy, and she too was called a bloodclat. Rainbow, in a huff, then left the flat, screaming vengeance from his blue lips.

He was alone with the sister. She was not a shy girl by any means and she turned her doleful eyes to him and here, sure enough, and now – yes – this was where the heart might be spoken of.

'Each morning,' she said, 'he'd wake me up with his dick in my back. That was lovely.' He was a skinhead, she said, and it was the first time ever she had been with one of those. Definitely it was love, she said, there was no question about that. She exhaled a heavy greenish smoke that lingered and he felt a tingle from her look.

'But then he start coming home later,' she said, 'didn't

he, and I'm, like, what the fuck? And was days he didn't come home at all. And nights. I said you got another an' she stashed someplace?'

Her features flashed a hard look as she revealed the skinhead's treachery.

'Turn out he was sticking his dick in more than one back,' she said. 'Turn out he couldn't keep it away from backs.'

As he sat and listened, as they smoked the weed together and sipped at their tins of Red Stripe, he found himself growing angry. It was the way that she kept talking about dicks.

'I'm not one of your girls,' he said at last.

'You what?'

'You're talking to me like I'm one of the girls,' he said. 'It's dick this, dick that, and dick the other. You're talking to me as if I don't have one myself. You're talking to me as if I'm not even here. You're talking to me as if I'm not even a possibility.'

'You're not,' she said.

'No?'

'You're depress',' she said.

He walked with the weed back to the terrace house. The Excelsior lager was busily washing down the gullies of the Connemara men a feed of chips and saveloys from the homicidal takeaway on the corner – someone had managed to walk. He had at this hour *presumed* the burp odour of low-grade meat products on the air, but even so it was a trial, and he sat among it feeling dickless and wild. The only way not to smell the saveloys was to eat one and quickly he succumbed.

'I'm after a run-in with a Jamaican bird,' he said. 'She had some arse on her now.'

The Connemara men ignored him. They watched a quiz show as they ate. There was heavy breathing in the room between mouthfuls, much too heavy for the ages of these men. Soon the heavy fug of the marijuana was laid atop the meat odour and also there was the sour tang of the Excelsior that was warming at the bottom of tins.

'She'd want to phone a friend here?'

'She would and all.'

'Tits on it?'

'Diddy wank.'

The babyish interest that was taken in the show was too much for him. He went to the bathroom out back for a wash and a think. He attempted to arouse himself with thoughts of Rainbow's sister but it would not take. Depress' is right, he said. He'd show the bitch depress' if he got a chance. No he wouldn't.

'Anyone for the Ducks?' he asked on returning to the room.

But there were no other takers for the local and he walked there alone. The dank streets of east London, in low January, and he trod a purposeful beat, with the shoulders held erectly, for show. The atmosphere at the Ducks as he entered its bar-room was rancorous.

'If you want me to stand up out of my seat,' growled an old Irish, 'then I'll do it, and I'll knock seven types of fucken shite out of you while I'm at it.'

The Irish wanted to watch the dog racing from Walthamstow on the satellite buy-in.

'You was born ignorant,' said an old West Indian. 'It's your poor wife I feel pain for. She deserve better. A good-lookin' lady. And she get hersel' a pig for a man.'

The West Indian wanted to watch the cricket from Barbados.

The breakdown across the bar-room of the Ducks was about evens. The clacking of dominoes from the West Indian tables; the slow slurping of mystic Guinness from the Irish. The barman, a baleful English, argued for compromise, for the dogs to be let on a while, then a switch.

'Don't surprise me,' the West Indian said, 'that you come back up the pig-man. He who come in here, with his red face . . .'

The West Indian stood then – he was most elegantly waistcoated, he was dapper.

'. . . he who come in here, in his *unpleasant* jacket.'

'Leave a man's clothes out of it,' the Irish said.

This would go on for the night, he knew, and so he moved through to the lounge, where the slot machine garbled and the pool balls conversed in great agitation. He bought a pint bottle of Magners – 'the taste of summer'– and he poured half of it to a glass filled with ice. The lounge began to fill up. The night was climbing up itself. One bottle gave onto the next; the first three were distinct, come the fourth they began to blur. The lounge was full of lively young creatures laden with trinkets and jaunty with menace. There was a bus organised for a nightclub in Essex. Eyes rolled up in their heads. The whites of eyes were everywhere conspicuous.

It was not so long until he was seeing double. Twice the shaven heads and twice the pool balls, and every image mirrored in the mirrors behind the bar was doubled again and he had to shut one eye tightly for the crowd to halve in number. It was in such a condition that he saw her come

108

across the lounge. The illusion held for the usual dream of a moment but then persisted. She broke through the field of his myopia and kept on coming. And then she was leaning down to him, there in his chair, in the lounge of the fucking Ducks, in fucking Leytonstone, and she was saying:

'Daniel?'

He wasn't sure about trying out some words. He opened the shut eye and the world threatened to double up again but to his relief it held.

'Ah Jesus,' he said, and he tried to make it sound as casual as possible.

She laughed and leaned closer again – he could smell her – and she kissed his cheek.

'I knew you were east somewhere,' she said, 'but Jesus!'

'What the fuck are you doing here?'

The shock of it sobered him. She pulled up a stool beside. She crossed her legs.

'My uncle died,' she said. 'He was Leyton?'

'Only down the road,' he said, and he ran a hand through his hair.

'I know,' she said. 'I just walked it with my cousins. How're you, Daniel?'

'It's like I'm trippin',' he said. 'On fucken mushrooms or something?'

'You're not still at that caper?' she said.

'Hardly,' he said. 'Since.'

'How've you been, Daniel?'

'Making steady progress, all told,' he said.

'Still a bit of a rocket, I'd say . . . Jesus, this is unreal!'

'It's bizarre,' he agreed.

She looked around, uncertainly:

'Who're you with?'

'I'm on my own.'

'Ah, Daniel, on a Saturday night?'

It was three whole months they had been together. Then she took the heart out of him and ate it.

'Jesus,' he said.

'And here we are,' she said.

'Daniel and Alicia,' he said. 'Long time since those names been seen in consort.'

'Consort!' she said. 'There you go with your words.'

'Well this is it,' he said.

'You're skinny,' she said. 'Are you looking after yourself?'

'Ah I am.'

'Where are you living?'

'Place called Matcham Road. Grand, just around the corner. Sharing a house there. It's grand.'

'Who're you sharing with?'

'Lads from Connemara,' he said.

'Uh-oh,' she said.

'Ah they're grand. They like their Excelsior.'

'Their what?'

'It's a hard lager. Super-strength. Come out of the can it's the colour of honey.'

'And you're working?'

'IT.'

'Good money?'

'Grand.'

'Are you okay, Daniel?'

'Why do you keep asking me am I fucken okay?'

'What, I'm sorry, it's just . . .'

'Just what, Lish?'

'You look sad.'

'Would you not be,' he said, 'when I'm seeing you every day?'

He hadn't sobered.

'When I see you come walking the street towards me and below in Stratford station and I see you in all the offices?'

'Daniel?' she said. 'What are you talking about?'

'I've seen you in the park,' he said. 'And I can't come home because I'll see you there for sure and I know you don't want me.'

'Ah Daniel.'

'And I don't want to put you out,' he said.

He leaned forward and sipped from his Magners. She wasn't getting up from that in a hurry.

'I've to go,' she said.

'Ah yeah.'

'We're going to a disco in Essex someplace.'

'Party bus,' he said. 'Massive.'

'Don't want to really, it's just my cousins.'

'Party bus,' he said, 'and the uncle still warm in the ground.'

'Daniel,' she said, 'you're so funny.'

She moved in and she kissed his cheek again and he closed his eyes.

'I'll see you around home sometime,' she said. 'Be careful!'

'Right so,' he said.

He drank his cider. The vision doubled on him again. Let them all off to their party bus. The bell rang for one more and he opened his eyes and stood uncertainly and he walked towards the bar. He didn't know how many Magners he was after.

The barman sucked his lips as though in warning as Daniel approached.

'You sure?'

'Listen,' Daniel said. 'Will you tell me something straight up please. Was I just talking to a girl there?'

'The black-haired piece?' the barman winced. 'Ooh. She was a sort. How's it you know her? She work community Outreach?'

'Okay,' said Daniel. 'Magners.'

'What about half a lager?'

'Better plan,' Daniel said.

He walked home a while later. What had earlier been clear sky had clouded over and now it was unseasonably mild. There was no gainsaying the past. With all else that had happened, he had held her too, and that could not be taken away. He turned in the gate of number 126 to see what way they were getting on inside with the Excelsior.

DOCTOR SOT

Late in January, Doctor Sot felt the bad headaches come on again and he drank John Jameson whiskey against them. The naggins slipped pleasingly into a compartment of his leather satchel but they needed frequent replacing and he thought it best not to replace them always from the same off-licence in town. He aimed the car for the 24-hour Tesco on the outskirts of town. A cold morning was coloured iron-grey on the hills above town – brittle and hard the winter had been, and it was such clear, piercing weather that brought on the headaches. The heater in his eleven-year-old Megane juddered bravely against the cold but inadequately and his fingers on the wheel had the look of a corpse's. Steady nips of the Jameson, he found, kept in check the visions of which these headaches were often the presage.

The Megane had a personality. It was companionable and long-suffering and he had named it Elizabeth for his mother. Car and mother had in common a martyr's perseverance and a lack of natural advantages.

'Small devil loose inside my head, Liz,' said Doctor Sot, 'and it's like he's scraping a blade in there, the little bastard.'

As he crossed the hump-back bridge over the White Lady's River he whistled the usual three-note sequence for luck, a bare melody, and he sucked in his cheeks against the pain. He groped inside the satchel for a naggin. He wedged the naggin between his thin thighs. He unscrewed the top and fate dug a pothole and the pothole caused the Megane to jolt. The jolt splashed whiskey onto the trousers of his Harris tweed.

'Oh thank you very much,' said Doctor Sot.

He checked the mirrors before raising the naggin. Clear. And it was just his own eyes in there, which was a relief. Mirrors, typically, were more troublesome for Doctor Sot earlier in the morning. He drained what was left of the whiskey and great vitality raged through him and he tossed the empty naggin in back.

'Another dead soldier, Liz,' he said, and with his grey lips he bugled a funeral death march.

The Tesco at eleven this weekday morning was quiet and the quietness for Doctor Sot had an eerie quality. As he walked the deserted aisles, wincing against the bright colours of the products, he felt like the lone survivor in the wake of an apocalypse. What would you do with yourself? All the fig rolls on earth wouldn't be a consolation. So taken was he with this grim notion he walked into a display of teabags and sent the boxes flying. He was upset to have knocked them and got down on his hands and knees to remake the stack in a neat triangle. He felt the hot threat of a urine seepage. He summoned his deepest reserves to staunch it – he was wearing, after all, his finest tweeds.

'Well this is a nice bag of sticks,' he said.

The seeping was tiny – a mercy – and the boxes of tea were at least in some manner restacked. He proceeded with as much nonchalance as he could muster. From the bakery counter he picked up a chocolate cake for his wife, Sal, who was the happiest woman alive. Also he placed in his basket some mouthwash, a family pack of spearmint gum and eight naggins of the John Jameson. A patient, Tim Lambert, appeared gormlessly around an aisle's turn with a duck-shaped toilet freshener in his hand.

'Tricks with you, Doctor O'Connor?' he enquired.

Doctor Sot put his basket on the floor and went into a boxer's swaying crouch. He jabbed playfully at the air around the old man's head.

'You're goin' down and you're stayin' down, Lambert!' he cried.

Tim Lambert laughed, and then he eyed, for the full of his mouth, the contents of the doctor's basket. Sot picked up the basket and primly moved on, the humour gone from him. The consolation was that Lambert's lungs wouldn't see out the winter – he had told no lie. Oh and he knew full well what they all called him behind his back. He knew it because another of his elderly patients, Rita Cryan, was gone in the head and had forgotten that the nickname was slanderous and meant to be secret.

'That's not a bad mornin' at all, Doctor Sot,' she always croaked when he paid a house call now. He tended with Rita to strap on the blood pressure monitor a little too tightly. There was temptation to open one of the naggins before he got it to the counter but he denied himself and bore the small devil's caper.

'You'd want a good class of a pelt on you,' he said to the girl at the till. 'Brass monkeys weather.'

But she was an eastern and as she blankly scanned his

115

items he realised that pelt was perhaps a little rich for her vocabulary, not to mind brass monkeys.

'Pelt like a bear,' he said. 'For the cold, I mean? Look it! Here's Papa Bear in his lovely warm pelt!'

He flapped his arms delightedly against his sides to indicate Papa Bear's cosiness.

'Is fifty-three euro eighty-nine cent,' she said.

In the Megane, he opened a naggin and he took a good nip for its dulling power. He saw a distressed van come coughing and spluttering into the car park. The rainbow colours it was painted in could not disguise the distress. It was driven by a young man with braided hair. Many small children, all shaven-headed, wriggled and crawled along the dashboard and against the windscreen. The man climbed down from the van and slid back the side door. More shaven-headed children poured out and more braided adults. These, Doctor Sot realised, must be the new-age travellers the paper had been on about. They were camped in the hills above town. On Slieve Bo, if he recalled. They were colourful and unclean and wore enormous military boots. There were bits of metal in their faces. They made a motley parade as they went across the car park. The driver remained at the side door of the van and spoke loudly to someone inside. A young woman poked her head out and spoke back to him. He huffed and he gestured and he followed the rest of the travellers across the car park. She remained. She stepped out and leaned against the van and rolled a cigarette from a pouch. Her hair also was in braids and piled high and she wore striped leggings tucked into her boots. Doctor Sot's breath caught as he watched her. She was remarkably beautiful and vital but there was something else that drew him, too. She felt his stare and returned it. She smiled and waved at him. Sot slugged hard on the naggin and took off.

There are wolves in our valley – this is what Doctor Sot knew. We do not know when they will attack us but attack us they surely will, with their hackles heaped and drool sheering from between their yellow teeth. The careful study of sickness had taken a great toll and weakened him but just a moment's view of the young woman had lifted him again to his calling, and Doctor Sot wasn't back across the White Lady's River before he had a plan formed.

The tinkers, those older travellers, held that the river's crossing was here auspicious because on the bank by the hump-back bridge was a may tree hundreds of years old and Doctor Sot, who would take all the luck from the world that he could get, whistled again his three notes as he crossed back into the town. His home and practice was on a neat terrace of greystone. It had been bought cheaply in the long-gone heyday of his practice. Having come from less – his persevering mother had put him in the university out of a council house – Doctor Sot enjoyed still the mild grandeur of his address. The three stone steps that led up to his door, the nine-panel fanlight above it, the fine parquet blocking of his hallway's floor, the blocks faded by the length of the years they had lived here; these were details that he greatly enjoyed. There was a bright, clean patch on the wall where a large gilt-edged mirror had lately been removed.

'Oh adieu! Yes adieu! Oh adieu all my false-hearted looooves!' sang Doctor Sot as he tap-danced through to the back kitchen, one hand flapping a minstrel's wave, the other clasping the satchel. Sal, in her gown, flushed and chortled at the sight of him – the only illusion of permanence is that which is finagled by love. She threw down her serial killer novel and bounced up from the small pink sofa by the stove.

'You'll never guess!' she cried. 'He's only taken the head and buried it in the desert!'

'This is the prostitute he met at the truckstop?'

'One and the same,' she whispered. 'Had the head in his fridge but it started to stink.'

'Neighbours might be alerted, Sal.'

'He's making a move to be on the safe side,' she said. 'He's headed for Tulsa. Ham sandwich, lovie?'

'It would fill a hole, Sal.'

'Your glass of beer with it?'

'Might take the fear of God off me.'

They embraced. Sot was stick and bone, Sally was hot and pink and fleshy.

'Mind you,' he said, 'I've a bit of a rush on. I need to make a call before surgery.'

'Oh?' she said. 'A call?'

She was already slicing the batch loaf. There weren't many calls these days.

'Health Board,' he said.

She opened the fridge for the ham, the butter, the can of Smithwick's. Happy as a duck she was, unshakable from her good humour, and of the opinion that her husband, if anything, grew more marvellous with every passing year.

'They're giving you gip again, dear-heart?'

'Not at all,' he said. 'It's just I've had a think about this Outreach programme.'

He sipped from the glass of beer she handed to him. He rubbed nervously a frayed tweed elbow.

'But they can't force you, Carl?'

118

'Of course not, my light. It's just I've thought maybe I was a little quick to rule it out . . . Maybe I should, you know, give something back?'

With his bloodshot eyes and his hammering heart! Doctor Sot hurried the beer, and he would leave the sandwich uneaten on the plate. He needed five minutes before surgery for the business with the mouthwash and the gum. His hurry would carve out another five for the call to the Health Board. As he downed the last of his beer, pain ripped the back of his skull. He went to the sink to block the wince from her. He squinted out and up to the white sky. The usual great wingéd creatures were taking shape for him up there. He turned quickly again to Sal.

'Service!' he cried. 'What ever happened to the notion of serving the people?'

'You know what, sweetness?'

Sal's mouth shaped with awe as she grasped the brilliance of his idea.

'It could be just the thing for you! Take you out of yourself!'

Whatever this heroically complicated husband came up with was fine with Sally. She quickly forgot the details of his frequent and disastrous adventures. Before he had even reached the phone in the hallway's nook, she was deep in the pink sofa and in the tale of her Tulsa-bound maniac: he was snacking on innards as he zoomed along the blacktop.

'Obviously, Carl, we're delighted you'd volunteer.'

'I'm sensing a but,' said Doctor Sot.

This Mahoney fellow at the Health Board was easy enough to read. All he wanted for Outreach was the young guns with the big grins and the surfer hair. Sot raged:

'Thirty-five years of experience! And I offer it up to you! I am offering, Mr Mahoney, to take part in your bloody Outreach programme. Just like you asked!'

'Carl, it was only a circular. Just a general call for volunteers. This was three months ago and really we've got it sorted now? All the halting sites are serviced. The seminars for the community centre are looked after. I've a couple of lads who've . . .'

'And our new-age travellers?' said Doctor Sot. 'Who's providing Outreach there?'

'You mean the crowd above on . . . Slieve Bo?'

That had him. Mahoney had to admit that the new-age travellers had not, in fact, been added to the Outreach list.

'Animals, are they, Mr Mahoney?'

'Oh I mean they'd qualify, I suppose, at least if they're receiving benefits but . . .'

'But but but, Mr Mahoney!'

It was agreed by sighing Mahoney that the new-age travellers would be assessed to see if they qualified for Outreach.

'In the meantime,' said Doctor Sot, 'it'd be no harm, surely, to go up there and show a friendly face? Just to introduce oneself? Maybe a few leaflets about nutrition? About chlamydia, that type of thing?'

'Whatever you think, Carl,' said Mahoney.

It was Doctor Sot's experience that the longer he stayed on the phone to people, the more he got what he wanted.

His surgery ran from noon until two. It was as slow as it always was now. Only the old and fatalistic still patronised the O'Connor practice. The lady of the Knotts whose twin had died in the winter was in about the voices again but the voices had turned benevolent and she was less disturbed

120

than she had been. Ellie Troy had that grey, heart-sick look but she was seventy-two now and she'd had the grey, heart-sick look since she was forty: it was a slow death for poor Ellie. It was the weather for sore throats, Doctor Sot told Bird Magahy. His own headaches weren't so bad during surgery and he was careful not to gaze out towards the white sky. Skies and mirrors – these were the fields of his visions, and oh, the strangenesses that he saw; hallucinations, yes, but no easier to handle for that. Last into surgery was Tom Feeney, the crane driver.

'It's the man below, Doctor O'Connor.'

'Do you mean, Tom . . .'

'I do.'

'He mightn't be doing all you'd require of him?'

'It's not that.'

'No?'

'It's the opposite of that.'

'Oh?'

'I'm in a state,' the sixty-year-old crane man said, 'of constant excitement.'

Doctor Sot prescribed a week's Valium and the taking up of a new hobby. He was in the back kitchen by five past two, kissing Sal, and telling her he was away on a mission.

'Outreach, Sal!'

'Bloody hell they've snapped you up quick enough!'

'I'll be back for the tea surely.'

'Careful how you go, honeybob!'

Over the bridge, a three-note whistle, and the main road he turned off for a side road. The side road became a boreen. The boreen as he climbed became track. Track became narrower track, and it turned onto a rutted half-track. It was like a path animals had trampled down. Suddenly space opened out on all sides and Doctor Sot steered his Megane through the air but she laboured, Elizabeth. The high country had its own feeling. Ascending into the iron-grey of its colours as the afternoon light fatted up, Doctor Sot was alerted to the different intensities of these greys and shale tones. Austere from below, they were radiant when you were up and among them. The higher reaches of the mountain were now everywhere open to him, the turloughs glistened coldly in the valley below, the gorse was seared to its winter bronze. The half-track hairpinned, and the travellers' camp was announced by a sudden assault of skinny dogs.

'Easy, Liz,' said Doctor Sot, as he steered the old girl through the dogs.

The camp was sheltered by a great outcrop of shale. High and wind-blown were the voices of perhaps a dozen shaven-headed children (their voices travelled) and as many again were the skinny dogs. The grown travellers skulked in the rearground, and were watchful; they came nearer. The children and dogs surrounded Doctor Sot as he climbed from the Megane. The ground was hard-packed underfoot, brittle and flinty; the frost wouldn't think to lift up here for months at a time. The children were pin-eyed and unpleasantly lively. The dogs might have been alien dogs, so skinny and yellow-skinned and long-headed they were, like bad-dream dogs, and they pawed him madly.

'Ah down off me now please! For the love of God!'

He might have landed in far Namibia such was the foreignness of things. There was something that resembled a teepee. Inside it was a generator, juddering. Sinister crows were

122

present in numbers. There were rough shelters made with lengths of tarpaulin and these were strewn around a copse of trees by the outcrop's base. There was a horse trailer with a smoking chimney. The distressed van of rainbow colours was parked beside it. There was a pair of old rusted caravans. The young chap who had earlier driven the van came through the barking children and the laughing dogs.

'S'about?' he said.

'Doctor Carl O'Connor!' cried Doctor Sot. 'North Western Health Board!'

'Oh yeah? I'm Joxie.'

'Outreach!' cried Doctor Sot. 'Welcome to Slieve Bo . . . Joxie?'

The young man swept back his mass of braided hair and arranged it away from his face. He was sharp-featured, sallow, bemused.

'I'm here about the nutrition,' said Doctor Sot. 'I'm here about the sex diseases.'

'You jus' piss yerself?' said Joxie.

More adults came forward. They swatted the children and kicked the dogs. A forest of braided hair sprang up around Doctor Sot but the beautiful young woman was not to be seen. He shielded his crotch with his satchel. Indeed there had been a tiny seepage.

'Aim of the Outreach programme,' he explained, 'is to bring the, ah . . . the services . . . to . . .'

He should have boned up on the stuff in the leaflets. He should have learned some of the lingo. But the travellers smiled at him regardless. They were not unwelcoming. Their accents were mostly English, the burr of them specifically south-western.

'Devon, so happens,' said Joxie.

He poured for Doctor Sot a cup of green tea. They were now in back of the horse trailer by a wood-burning stove. The young man's full title, it emerged, was Joxie The Rant.

'Rant, Joxie? Why so?'

''Coz I get a rant on,' he said. 'A ranter, yeah?'

'Do him a rant, Jox!'

'Bit early, is it no?'

The adults of the camp were greatly taken with Doctor Sot. There were six of them packed into the trailer around him. He was a break from the boredom – the boredom that was bred into them by suburbs and drab English towns. Doctor Sot found it difficult to tell them apart, even to sex them, but he knew well enough that the beauty was not here. There was muffled hilarity to the brief silences that yawned out between them. To fill these, he spoke of the importance of five portions daily of fresh fruit and veg.

'Your broccoli is a powerful man,' he said. 'Handful of florets? There's a portion, there's one of your five.'

He spoke of oily fish, such as mackerel, for the sake of its Omega 3.

'Ground control to Omega 3,' said Joxie.

The travellers smoked their roll-ups and drank green tea. As this was not an official Outreach session, as it was more of a break-the-ice visit, Doctor Sot saw no reason why he shouldn't offer to strengthen their tea. He opened the satchel and with a wink produced a full naggin.

'Nip of this lad?' he whispered. 'Greatly medicinal.'

'They do know yer out an' about, yeah?' said Joxie.

The evening began to flow. By the time a second naggin had

gone around, the travellers had in their civility produced tins of own-brand supermarket lager and flagons of unlabelled cider. They questioned Doctor Sot as to what pills he might have in his satchel. He laughed them away.

'It's the six, just, is it?' he tried. 'Just the six of you, for grown-ups?'

'Well there's Mag an' all, ain't there?' said Joxie. 'Mag's in her bender.'

'Oh?'

'She got one of her spells on, don't she?' said Joxie.

'Spells?' Sot asked.

There was no reply, and Sot fretted. He drank to brace himself. And he drank more quickly. And quickly it was as if Doctor Sot had become part of the camp – the travellers largely forgot about him. They were in and out of the horse trailer, attending to children and dogs. They smoked their roll-ups with a resin crumbled in. They sipped at their lager and cider. They didn't say no to another nip of the Jameson – Doctor Sot fetched extra from Elizabeth – but their conversation was no longer centred on the visitor. They talked drowsily about making some dinner. They talked about how they were going to get the van sorted. They talked, at some length, of the significance of the number '23'.

'Why have the children no hair?' asked Doctor Sot.

'Nits,' said Joxie.

Joxie tugged up the sleeves of his army shirt to show Doctor Sot the abscesses that had formed around old needle holes. Doctor Sot said that he'd be as well to come down to the practice and there they could have a closer look, there would be no charge for it. He said if anyone else needed to come down, that could also be arranged. Joxie decided to rant. One of the hanks of hair battered some tom-tom drums, and Joxie launched into a half-sung, half-shouted diatribe. It was all Greek to Doctor Sot, though he recognised that there were repeated references to 'Jah Rastafari', the number '23', and, more aggressively, to 'George Bush'.

Evening came among them. Doctor Sot sat back in the trailer and, woozily, he faded into and from the moment. A hand placed before him a saucer of curried vegetables.

'A wonderful idea,' he said.

He ate the food. It put sense in him. Mag had not appeared, and so he picked up his satchel. The dogs and children and adults were all around him in the dark as he clambered into the Megane.

'It's, ah . . . it's been an education,' said Joxie.

They all laughed, Doctor Sot as hard as the rest of them, and indeed until he wept. His eyes were full of tears as he started up Elizabeth. He immediately drove her into a ravine. He sobered at once, with the impact, and the travellers helped him from the car. It was the end of the eleven-year-old Megane – its remains fumed slowly in the dark, the smoke of its last breaths rose in a dense tangling. Gingerly, Sot fetched out the rest of the naggins and the chocolate cake that he had bought earlier for Sal but had forgotten to give her. He sat on the hard-packed soil of the camp, with a handkerchief held to his bleeding head.

'Poor Liz,' he sighed. 'Poor Sal.'

There was some of the relief that accompanies an old parent's death.

'Hell we gonna do with you?' said Joxie.

'Perhaps you'd run me down the mountain, Joxie,' Sot said. 'Your van?'

'No lights,' Joxie said.

It would be next morning before he could be brought down safely. He would need to stay the night. The travellers found their way around the camp's darkness by the glow of their mobile phones. Each was a pin-prick of light against the mountain black. He used his own phone to call Sal.

'Darling?' he said. 'There's some bad news. I'm afraid it's Elizabeth . . .'

Sal was not at all worried that he was caught out on Slieve Bo. She was well used to his capers and disappearances. Often, Doctor Sot was gone for days at a time. Many was the ditch of the north-west he had woken up in. Once he woke beneath an upturned rowing boat on the shore of Lough Gill – one leg of his trousers had been entirely wet, the other entirely dry. He had never quite pieced that one together. Tonight's accommodation wasn't bad at all. He was shown into one of the rusted caravans. The travellers turned out to be early-to-bed types: the boredom. By nine, there were no lights at all but those dim cold ones hung in the sky above. Bald children and alien dogs stretched around the caravan with him and they all slept sweetly. Doctor Sot could not settle, but sat. He drew on a naggin and looked out to the camp. The chocolate cake, uneaten, was on his lap in its white box. His eyes adjusted to the dim, eerie glow of the starlight as it made shapes inside the caravan – the prone figures of the kids and the dogs, breathing. Sot stood then and he approached bravely a mirror mounted on the door of a cupboard. He crept up on it, carefully, and found that it was clear – no malevolence – and he backed away. He crept up on it again and still it was clear – no malevolence – he backed away. He crept up a third time and a figure appeared in the mirror but there was no malevolence – it was his young woman, outside. She looked in at him. She made not a move, but smiled. He climbed down from the caravan and went to her. The serenity in her smile, it was confirmed at once, was that of a psychotic.

'Ya wanna see my bender?' she said.

'I'd love to, Mag,' said Doctor Sot.

'Knows my name 'n' all,' she said.

The bender was on the one side a length of tarp stretched over a run of willow branches staked in the ground. The other side was walled by the shale outcrop and on this Mag had sketched drawings of great wingéd creatures and a series of mathematical equations.

'Soon's I get 'em right,' she said, 'I paints over an' I start again.'

'You're bringing forward knowledge each time, Mag,' he consoled.

The bender was warmed by a tiny pot-belly stove, its flue extended through a hole in the tarp. The bender was lit barely by a battery lamp and it had pallets for flooring.

'Ya wan' yer pallets down,' she said. 'With yer pallets down, the damp it don't get up.'

'The way to go, Mag, unquestionably. We don't want the damp getting up.'

'Thing is,' she said. 'Soon's ya get yer pallets down, get yer rats run under, dontcha? So what I've done?'

She stuck her head out the bender's slit and tugged at Doctor Sot's arm so that he did the same.

'Chicken wire,' she said. 'I've closed off space between pallets, haven't I? Means no rat run.'

'There's peace of mind in that, Mag.'

They had cake. She showed him in detail her equations. Mag, he learned, was involved in divining the true nature of time and memory. She believed that each of these ungraspable entities ran in arcs, and that the arcs bent away from each other. She had concluded this after long study of her staked willow branches. The diverging nature of these arcs was the source of all our ills. She might be onto something there, thought Doctor Sot. He wasn't sure where she was getting the figures for her equations from. Perhaps they were being carried to Slieve Bo in the talons of the great wingéd creatures.

'Do you take medication at all, Mag?'

'Poisons? Hardly,' she said.

'Nip of this, Mag?'

'Nah,' she said. 'Don't agree with me.'

They sat beside each other with their backs to the shale. She drew up a blanket over her striped legs and offered him some of it. He took a piece and raised it to his face to smell it. It was the smell of a child's blanket: stale rusk and hot milk.

'Do you sleep, Mag?'

'In daylight more so,' she said.

But after a time her eyes did close. Doctor Sot slid a hand from beneath the blanket and lightly, very lightly, he laid it against her face. He felt the tiny fires that burned there beneath her skin. Her lashes were unspeakably lovely as they lay closed over her light sleep. If Doctor Sot could draw into his palm these tiny fires and place them with his own, he happily would.

Down in the valley the blackbirds were singing against the winter dark. The White Lady's River ran calmly beneath the hump-back bridge and past the may tree whose blossom would in late spring protect us. The town slept, but in the back kitchen of the terrace house he knew that Sally was on her pink sofa yet. Dear Sal – her gown, her grin, her mad thyroidal eyes. She rose from the sofa and went calmly on a tour of the house. She flowed through the house. For fear that he would get back early, she would lay cloths now over all the mirrors in the house.

THE GIRLS AND THE DOGS

I was living in a caravan a few miles outside Gort. It was set up on breeze blocks in the yard of an old farmhouse. There were big nervous dogs outside, chained. Their breathing caught hard with the cold of the winter and the way the wind shuddered along their flanks was wretched to behold. I lay there in the night, as the dogs howled misery at the darkness, and I doted over a picture of my daughter, May-Anne, as she had been back in the summertime. I hadn't seen her in eight months and I missed her so badly. I was keeping myself well hidden. Things had gone wrong in Cork and then they went wronger again. I had been involved with bringing some of the brown crack in that was said to be causing people to have strokes and was said to have caused the end altogether of a prostitute lad on Douglas Street. Everybody was looking for me. There was no option for a finish only to hop on a bus and then it was all black skies and bogger towns and Gort, finally, and Evan the Head waited for me there, in the ever-falling rain, and he had his bent smile on.

'Here's another one I got to weasel you out of,' he said. 'And me without the arse o' me fuckin' kecks, 'ay?'

He jerked a thumb at a scabby Fiesta that wore no plates and we climbed into it and we took off through the rain,

January, and we drove past wet fields and stone walls and he asked me no questions at all. He said it was often the way that a fella needed a place and he would be glad to help me out. He said that I was his friend after all and he softened the word in his mouth – friend – in a way that I found troubling. It was the softness that named the price of the word. He said things could as easily be the other way around and maybe someday I would be there to help him out. We turned down a crooked boreen that ran between fields left to reeds and there were no people anywhere to be seen. We came to the farmhouse and the smile on the Head's face twisted even more so.

I never promised you a rose garden, he said.

You would have hardly thought it held anyone at all but for the yellow screams of children escaping the torn curtains and the filthy windows. Evan said he had rent allowance got for the house on account of his children. He had bred six off Suze and a couple off her sister, Elsie. These were open-minded people I was dealing with. At least with regard to that end of things. We went inside and the kids appeared everywhere, they were shaven-headed against the threat of nits, and they were pelting about like maniacs, grinding their teeth and hammering at the walls, and the women appeared – girlish, Elsie and Suze, as thin as girls – and they smirked at me in a particular way over the smoke of their roll-ups: it is through no fault of my own that I am considered a very handsome man.

'Coffee and buns, no?' said Evan the Head, and the girls laughed.

The house was in desperate shape. There were giant mushroomy damp patches coming through the old wallpaper and a huge fireplace in the main room was burning smashed-up chairs and bits of four-be-two. The Head wasn't lying when he said I'd be as well off outside in the caravan. He brought me to it and I was relieved to get out to the yard, mainly because of the kids, who had a real viciousness to them.

Now of course the caravan was no mansion either. The door's lock was busted and the door was tied shut with a piece of chain left over from the dogs and fixed with a padlock. The dogs were big and of hard breeds but they were nervous, fearful, and they backed away into the corners of the yard as we passed through. Evan unlooped the chain and opened the door and with a flourish bid me enter.

'Can you smell the sex off it?' he said, climbing in behind.

'Go 'way?'

'Bought it off a brasser used to work the horse fairs,' he said. 'If the walls could talk in this old wagon, 'ay?'

It had a knackery look to it sure enough. It was an old sixteen-footer aluminium job with a flowery carpet rotten away to fuck and flouncy pillows with the flounce gone out of them and it reeked of the fields and winter. There was a wee gas fire with imitation logs. Evan knelt and got it going with his lighter.

'Get you good an' cosy,' he said. 'You any money, boy-child?'

'I've about three euro odd, Ev.'

'Captain of industry,' he said.

The gas fire took and the fumes rose from it so hard they watered my eyes. I asked was it safe and he said it'd be fine, it'd be balmy, it'd be like I was on my holidays, and if I got

133

bored I could always pop inside the house and see if young Elsie fancied a lodger.

'For her stomach,' he said.

I am not lying when I tell you there was a time Evan the Head was thought to be a bit of a charmer. He was from Swansea originally and sometimes in his cups he would talk about it like it was a kind of paradise and his accent would come through stronger. I had known him five years and I would have to say he was a mysterious character. I had met him first in a pub on Barrack Street in Cork called the Three Ones. It wasn't a pub that had the best of names for itself. It was a rough crowd that drank there and there was an amount of dealing that went on and an amount of feuds on account of the dealing. There had been shootings the odd time. I was nervous there always but Evan was calm and smiling at the barside and one night I went back to the flat he had in Togher and I bought three sheets of acid off him at a good price – White Lightnings, ferocious visuals – and he showed me passports for himself that were held under three different names. I was young enough to be impressed by that though I have seen quarer sights since, believe me. Evan used to talk about orgies all the time. He would go on and on about organising a good proper orgy – 'ay? – and he told me once about an orgy in a graveyard in Swansea that himself and an old girlfriend had set up and that's when he started taking down Aleister Crowley books about the occult and telling me he suspected I might be a white witch.

Magick, said Evan, should be always written with the extra 'k'.

I emptied out my bag in the caravan – it held just a few

pairs of boxer shorts and T-shirts and trackie pants. I had little enough by way of possessions since Fiona Condon had turfed me out, the lighting bitch. I had not arranged to collect my stuff. I would not give her the satisfaction, her and her barring order, and I was dressing myself out of Penney's. She hadn't let me near my daughter; I hadn't seen May-Anne since that day in early summer I had taken her out to the beach at Garrettstown. Evan watched me as I unpacked my few bits and I felt by his quietness that he was sorrowful for me. At least I hoped that was what the quietness was.

'Have you any food, Ev?' I said.

'You not eaten?'

I told him I'd made it from Cork on the strength of a banana and a Snickers bar.

'Poor starving little wraith,' he said.

He said I could come in later. He said there would be a pot of curried veg on the go. And that was the way our routine began. I would come in, the evenings, and I would be fed, and I would watch TV for a while and help with burning the four-be-twos before going and dry-humping Elsie on a mattress in a back room that smelled of kid piss and dried blood.

Elsie the third night told me that she loved me.

Now Elsie to this day I do not believe had original badness in her. It was just that she could be easily led and her sister had badness in her sure enough and as for Evan, well.

I said, the third night:

'But Elsie you're fleadhin' Ev and all, yeah?'

'What's fleadhin'?' she said.

'Fuckin',' I said. 'It's a Cork word for fuckin'.'

135

'Business o' yours how?' she said.

Elsie and Suze were from Leeds – Leeds-Irish – and they had people in south Galway. Their father had been put away for knocking their mother unconscious with the welt of a slap hammer and they turned up on the doorstep of the Galway cousins and they were turned away again lively. Their eyes were too dark and their mouths were too beautiful. They were the kind of girls – women – who look kind of dramatic and unsafe. They were at a loose end arsing around Galway then, fucking Australians out of youth hostels and robbing them, and they met Evan the Head in the Harbour Bar, was the story, when there still was a Harbour Bar, before the Galway docks was all cunts in pink shirts drinking wine. Evan was loaded at that time having brought in a trawler full of grade-two resin from Morocco – he came into Doolin with it, bold as brass, stoned as a coot in the yellow of his oilskins – and that was ten years back and if one of the sisters wasn't up the spout off him since, the other was.

'Evan an' me is over,' said Elsie, 'but I'm not sayin' he isn't a wonderful father.'

At that moment there was the loud cracking sound of wood snapping – *shhlaaack!* – which meant that Evan the Head had lain a length of four-be-two along the bottom steps of the stairs and taken a lep at it from the banister. He was a limber man and he enjoyed breaking up the firewood in this way.

See him perched up on the banister, with the weird grin on, and he eyeing just the spot where he wanted to crack the wood – then the wee lep.

In Cork I had seen Suze sure enough, lumbering under

children and dope smoke on the couch of the Togher flat, but I had never seen Elsie though I had heard her, once, in a far room, crying.

'Does Suze love him still do you think?'

'No,' said Elsie, 'but he has the spell on her, don't he? I can beat the spell.'

So it was – so simple – that we became a kind of family that January in the old farmhouse outside Gort. But of course I could not say I was ever entirely comfortable with the situation. I kept going out to the caravan at night, to be alone for those cold hours, for my own space and to think of May-Anne, to look at her photograph, and to listen to the dogs, the strange comfort of them. Elsie thought this was snobbish of me. She wanted me to stay with her on the mattress. And Evan the Head said he agreed with her, and Suze agreed, and that was the start of the trouble.

But I'm getting ahead of myself. I want to tell you about Elsie and what she looked like when she came. She wouldn't allow me to put it inside because there'd been complications with the last child she'd had bred off her for Evan and she didn't want another kid happening. I said fine to that. I have never been comfortable with being a father. I love May-Anne – my dotey pet, I always call her – but it makes me frightened just to think of her walking around in the world with the people that are out there. See some of the fuckers you'd have muttering at the walls down around the bus station in Parnell Place, Cork. You'd want a daughter breathing the same air as those animals?

'Get in there!' Ev cried from the hallway into the back room where Elsie and I lay on the mattress. 'Get in!'

When she came Elsie had a tic beneath her left eye – at

the top of her cheek there was a fluttering as if a tiny bird was caught beneath her skin. The dry-humping made me feel like a teenager again but not in a good way. We lay there – a particular night – with Elsie's tic going, with me all handsome and useless, and Evan leapt on the four-be-twos off the banister, and the eight mad kids bounced off the ceilings and bit each other and screamed, and the wind howled outside, and the wretched dogs cried a great howling in answer to the wind, and then Suze was at the door, and she said:

'Why don't we make this interestin'?'

Yes it started like that – the trouble – it started as a soft kind of coaxing. Sly comments from Suze and sly comments from Evan the Head. And I got worried when the winter stretched on, the weeks threw down their great length, the weeks were made of sleet and wind, and it became February – a hard month – and the sly comments came even from Elsie then. She was easily led and bored enough for badness. I started to feel a bit trapped in this place and I thought about moving on but I had nowhere to go and no money to get there. Given the way things had turned out in Cork, I would be shot or arrested if I went back, no question. I missed May-Anne so badly but I thought the best I could do for her was to keep myself safe until the troubled times had passed over.

Then, late one night, Evan the Head came into the yard – I heard him hiss at the dogs – and without so much as a knock he was in the door of the caravan and he sat on the foot of my fold-out bed. He lit a candle and I saw him by its soft light. He had his twisted smile on. First words he said to me:

'Suze is the better comer.'

'Go 'way?'

'Know what a geyser is?'

'I do, yeah.'

'That's Suze if she's in the form. You see she's got one eye a dark brown and one a dark, really dark green?'

'Yeah, kinda . . .'

'Yeah kinda noticed that, 'ay? Did you, boy?'

'Yeah.'

'Yeah well that's a good sign,' he said, 'for a comer.'

I did not reply because I did not like the way he was smoking his roll-up. The hard little sucks on it and his eyes so deep-set.

'She's inside,' he said.

I said nothing.

'I said she's waitin' on you, boy. Are you goin' to keep her waitin'?'

'Ah please, Ev.'

'You don't want to get that lady riled. Suze? Not a good plan, boy-child. I said you don't get that fucking lady riled.'

'Evan, look, I've the thing with her sister, haven't I?'

He stood then – he loomed in the candlelight – and the words that came were half spat, half whispered:

'You'll get in that fucking house and you'll fuck my wife and you'll fuck her sister or you'll get the fuckin' life taken out of you, d'ya hear me, boy?'

'Evan get out of the caravan, please!'

He leapt up on the bed then and he danced about and he laughed so hard. And he kind of poked at my head with his feet, kind of playful, as if he was going to stamp me, but he let it go, he stood down, and he left without another word. Then I heard him turn the padlock on the chain outside.

They kept me locked in the caravan for days and nights I quickly lost the count of. The windows were rusted shut and could not be squeezed back and I was so weak because they brought me no food and no water. I was in a bad state very quickly. The dogs outside I believe sensed that I was weakening, that I was dying, and they called to me. We were held on the same length of chain. In the daytime the girls came and whispered through the door to me – awful, filthy stuff that I would not repeat, for hours they whispered – and I knew that Elsie hadn't the better of the spell anymore. Evan came by night and he crawled over the roof of the caravan and he made little tapping noises. I roared and cried myself hoarse but there was no one to hear me out there and after a few days I was slipping in and out of a desperate weird sleep – full of sour, scary dreams, like bad whiskey dreams – and I felt the cold of the fields come into my bones and once in the afternoon dusk I woke from a fever to find Evan the Head outside a window of the caravan and in each of his arms he held a child to look in at me, and I knew it was the first time ever that I had seen those children calm. I have never had religion or spiritual feelings but lying there in the caravan in the farmyard outside Gort I knew for sure there was no God but there was surely a devil.

But if I gritted my teeth against the fear and kept my eyes clamped tightly shut, the sweats would seem to ease off for a while and I would see clearly my day on the beach with May-Anne, at Garrettstown, in the summer. It was a windy, blustery day, but the sea and the sand made us high, we were soaring, and we ran about like mad things on the beach. Afterwards, before the bus back to town, I bought her a 99 at a seaside shop. The shop had all sorts of beach tat for sale and she asked me about the pork-pie hats that said 'kiss-me-quick'.

'What's kiss-me-quick?'

'It's just a seaside thing,' I said. 'An old saying. From England I think.'

'Kiss-me-quick kiss-me-quick kiss-me-quick,' she said it in a duck's voice from a cartoon and I pecked her on the cheek, really quickly, peck peck peck, and I nuzzled the nape of her neck – she squealed.

I don't know how many days I had been locked in the caravan when I crawled the length of it one morning and under the sink found two tins of Campbell's Cream of Tomato Soup from years ago, probably – from the days of the brasser I would say. I opened them and I drank them cold and if I did not come to life exactly it felt as if my thoughts came for a short while in a clearer, more realistic way. Then I went to the closet to throw up.

I hated to use the chemical toilet in there because of the smell but I had no choice – my gut heaved and emptied itself. I wrapped myself around the tiny plastic loo, tears streaming. I saw then that the spillage over the years had worked away at the floorboards beneath. They were rotten to the extent that some had been replaced with a piece of ply.

I waited until the night. Elsie and Suze had come out just once in the afternoon to whisper their filth at me, and Evan had on the roof for a while made his tap-tappings and I believed he was working at some kind of spell – something from an Aleister Crowley book, maybe; magick – and when he went away I waited, waited, until all in the farmhouse was darkness and quiet, and there was just the feeling of the dogs outside.

I unhooked the chemical loo and lifted it clear and the ply beneath came loose so easily it was unreal, it was like wet cardboard in my hands. The hole I quickly made was no more than two, two and a half foot wide but that was enough to squeeze through, and I scraped past an axle, and I was crawling along the wet ground of the yard then beneath the caravan. All of the dogs huddled close to the ground and peered at me, oh and their eyes – so yellow – were livid, but they made not a sound, they were quiet as the air was cold.

I wriggled out from beneath the caravan and sat with my back to it to ease the beating of my heart. No lights came on in the farmhouse and the dogs in perfect silence watched me as I found the strength to walk to the Fiesta and climbed into it. I lifted off the panel for the wires to come loose and I knew well enough which wires to rub together.

I was no more than halfways down the crooked boreen when the lights came on in the farmhouse and there were roars and screams and the sound of doors and footsteps and with my eyes pinned ahead I steered along till the boreen gave onto road and I missed the verge and the tyre ripped on rocks but I kept going hard into the night. The way the ripped rubber of the tyre slapped along the back road had a rhythm to it – three beats, again and again and again – and I heard it as kiss-me-quick, kiss-me-quick, and I drove it until the screaming of the voices – oh May-Anne – and all that was behind me had faded – my sweetheart, my dotey – to nothing, just nothing at all, and I was at a high vantage suddenly and beneath me, on a plain, were the lights of Gort.

WHITE HITACHI

The next thing was he had to get the van out of the clampers. He walked out there past the industrial estate and the traffic was all eyes: he felt as if they were all watching him – who's the latchiko on the hoof?

And of course up top of the situation with the van was the situation with Enya's father. The father had put word out that the next time he saw Patrick Mullaney he was going to take the head clean out of his shoulders. Patrick had not known that Enya was only fifteen and a half years of age. It wasn't as if she was small – there was no shortage of the girl. And it was only the one date they'd had. He took her to an Apache Pizza on the by-pass road and they shared a Meat Supreme. She wouldn't get in the back of the van so he drove her to a Topaz station and they had sex in the handicapped toilet there. To delay climax, he had focused on the toilet cleaning schedule pinned to the wall. It claimed with biro signatures that some buck called Felim had cleaned the toilet at hourly intervals all day until 6 p.m. and a girl called Marnia had done the job at 7 p.m., 8 p.m., 9 p.m. She did in my hole, Patrick thought, looking at the filth of the stall around him. Enya moaned softly meantime and she had been no stranger to such moans was Patrick Mullaney's belief.

As he walked out to the clampers, he worried less about the father and more that Enya might have a bad memory of their night together. He shook free of the worry by telling himself Enya hadn't seemed like the remembering kind.

Once he got the van back, and presuming he stayed blindside of Enya's father, the plan was to spring Tee-J from the juvenile detention unit. Not spring, exactly – that was just Patrick's dramatic way of telling things to himself. Tee-J was officially due for release – he had served the full six months. Tee-J (who sometimes spelled it T-Jay, who had his head wet Thomas John) was his younger brother. Teedge, Patrick usually called him, to the boy's annoyance. Teedge had done the six months after robbing an Isuzu Trooper that belonged to a guard's wife and driving it through three counties. He was followed all the while by the same guard until the guard hit a ditch. Was said that coming out of Elphin the Isuzu had clocked the third highest speed ever recorded in County Roscommon. Fucking legend, Tee-J, in Patrick's book, and barely seventeen. But there had to be an end to it.

Patrick was himself thirty-six, if it's ages we're on about. Which should be old enough to know better and which did not make him feel good about the fact that after getting the van out of the clampers and avoiding Enya's father and springing (so to speak) Tee-J from the juvenile detention unit, he was going to have to call around to Doggie Mannion's place and offload three hundred and fifty-nine DVDs and a wire cutters. Provided they were still under the boards in the back of the van. It was the only move he could make. Better to turn them over to The Dog – for a euro a pop, if he was lucky – than have them lying around the van. If and when he got the van out of the clampers. He fingered for the fiftieth time the roll of notes in the pocket of his jeans. There was two-seventy euro and change to his name and he was well aware that the clampers usually took a three-ton release fee, minimum.

He tried to avoid the eyes of the traffic. Fuckers in pink shirts with big pink heads in their Saabs and the suit jackets all neat behind the drivers' seats on hangers. He noted that people threw rubbish around like it was going out of fashion, coffee cups, chicken boxes, and this got him down.

An Alsatian behind a chain-link fence lost the rag as Patrick passed and he eyeballed the dog.

'Kkksssssst!' he said to it.

There were going to be some changes. He was determined that Patrick and Tee-J were on the straight and narrow from this day forward. Yes sir. There would be no more ferreting DVDs out of Enniskillen warehouses, no more county records in Isuzu Troopers, no more messing around in handicapped toilets with Enyas out of transition years. They had been through enough of the rough times.

Now of course more or less everybody was dead. The mother, the father, the two sisters, another brother, uncles, aunts, cousins coming out the wazoo, a rake of buddies – dead dead dead, or at least mostly, and if they weren't dead, they were in Castlerea prison, or the secure ward at the madhouse (many a Mullaney had bothered the same walls), or gone to England. The droning of the traffic beside him as he reached now the clampers' yard was much of a muchness with the droning of his dead's babble.

In some ways, Patrick felt he was doing well by Tee-J. For a nice stretch there, he had the boy set up with his own bedroom in an executive apartment overlooking the

Shannon. A good seven-fifty square foot of a job, with French doors out to a balcony, an extractor hood, power shower, underfloor heating.

'We're fartin' through silk here, Teedge.'

'You ain't tellin' no lies, Patch.'

He was in the other of the two bedrooms. He'd lie plumb in the middle of the bed and lay out his limbs as though he was doing a starjump. It was a golden period in their lives even if it wasn't their own apartment, technically speaking. He had gained access to it by the balcony. They had found a woman's swimsuit on the balcony. It would have been from the summer previous and it had been forgotten and the freshwater she must have swam in had dried the river slime into it and had left it stiff. That blasted Shannon must have been crawling with the dirt altogether, was Patrick's feeling. He was concerned also, for a reason he could not name, at the way Tee-J handled the swimsuit and was fascinated by it and the way the boy kept taking it back out of the pedal bin.

All of the apartments at the complex were empty that season and they had a prize November there. They had watched box sets of DVDs and eaten pizza every night and they kept the heating on full blast. Of course it couldn't last and the Ukrainians had shown up with tyre irons soon enough. What class of a security operation is it that sends fellas around to you with tyre irons and they babbling their gobbledy-gook and big ignorant pusses on them? That was what Patrick Mullaney wanted to know. Tee-J was all for going toe-to-toe with the Ukrainians, no better man, but Patrick knew there was no odds in that and there you had it – they were living out of the white Hitachi.

Again.

They drove it to quiet places all the winter through. Was the time they drove it out past Boyle and into the hills and came up past the forestry land and along to Keash – there were caves up there. Caves, if you don't mind. They parked the Hitachi and climbed up and they had a good look around the caves. They thought about it. A sign put up for tourists told them that a high king of Connaught had been raised and cared for in the caves by she-wolves.

'Blow job off one a them and you'd know all about it,' said Tee-J.

'A low-class remark,' said Patrick.

An unspoken fear he had was that Tee-J would at some point kill. They read that hunter-gatherers of olden times had used the caves for shelter when they were on expedition.

'Are we huntin' and gatherin'?' said Tee-J.

'Are we what,' said Patrick.

Caves was a crazy notion so they ended up doing time at a crustie camp outside Manorhamilton. The crusties had a crop of magic mushrooms not long dried and they were decent enough about handing them out. Of course that got hairy quick when Tee-J started having apparitions of the dead mother in back of the Hitachi. Who was the last bitch on the planet you wanted to see coming back. So that was enough with the mushrooms. Next thing Patrick took a wrong signal off one of the crustie women and dropped a hand that shouldn't have been dropped. That ended up in a row involving a crowbar and a fella with dreadlocks from Gloucester and a three-legged pitbull.

Good luck, Manorhamilton.

They went east as far as Longford and did some work for a retard farmer there. Poor buck had that shaking disease and couldn't hammer fence posts no more. Three days was as long as the brothers had lasted at the fence posts themselves.

'What are we, blacks?' said Tee-J.

There was no rent allowance being given if you hadn't an address to claim it out of. The woman at the social said there was a caravan park in Sligo was taking temporaries all the year round if they were stuck.

'Do we look like tinkers to you?' said Patrick Mullaney.

Inside in a coffee shop in Carrick one morning he had been struck by the solidity of its walls. When you were sleeping in lay-bys, in the Hitachi, and if a good wind got up at all, the walls gave and returned like a melodeon. Patrick found himself patting the coffee-shop walls and thinking: Jesus but that's solid out. Wasn't long after Tee-J took the notion of flaking off with the guard's wife's Isuzu Trooper.

Of course the buck in the kiosk at the clampers had a face on him like a dose of cancer.

''Bout a white Hitachi,' said Patrick.

'I'd say 'tis.'

''Twas taken in illegal.'

'I'd say 'twas.'

'I was only gone into the doctor's with my daughter. She has spina bifida. I have the handicapped sticker alright but it's lost. I had to carry her home in my arms.'

'Three hundred even.'

'The van isn't worth that.'

'Not my problem, son.'

'I don't have three hundred.'

149

'Not my problem. Your problem.'

'If the wind changes that face will stick on you.'

'If you're going to be abusive you can leave the way you came.'

'I want to speak to the manager.'

'Hello good evening and welcome. Three hundred and you're on the road.'

'Ye're licensed by the council, ye are? Council know this the way ye're treating fathers of spina bifada children?'

'Much have you on you?'

So it was that when he was hauling into the juvenile detention unit he didn't even have the price of a bottle of Coke for Tee-J. The better news was that there was three-quarters of a tank of petrol and the DVDs were still under the boards. Imagine, he thought, if you did have a child with spina bifida? He was sobbing uncontrollably by the time he parked the Hitachi in the visitors' car park.

Wiped the tears away as he crossed the car park and the summer sky was white and massive and it made him feel headachey, out of sorts, clairvoyant.

Patrick Mullaney could tell you this much for nothing: there wasn't anything good coming.

Tee-J was waiting in the reception area with some class of a supervisor, a glorified swing-key except the swing-keys wore baby blue polo shirts in this place and smiled all the time. There were rapist young fellas playing pitch 'n' putt in these places.

Tee-J wouldn't even make eye contact with his one remaining brother.

Tee-J turned to the polo shirt as Patrick approached and he said:

'You can tell this cunt to go sling his huke.'

'Ah Teedge . . .'

Tee-J had outpaced the guard till the guard hit the ditch and he wound up sitting on the bonnet of the Isuzu Trooper in Strandhill and looking out over the sea smoking a fag like he was off a film. Of course the guards knew full well who it was they'd been chasing – Mullaneys in this neck of the country were in no need of identikit mock-ups. Patrick had had a bad feeling about Tee-J around that time. The daft child had a black-moon look about the eyes and Patrick reckoned if the Teedge wasn't held safe behind bars, he was going to be toes up on a slab with the hair parted wrong. So he turned his own brother in and that felt so like it was off a film he almost heard the music strike up on the soundtrack.

The polo shirt was all in a flutter – loving it – as he tried to bring the brothers together. Patrick wondered if they weren't all half-steamers working in these places.

'Teedge, it was for your own good, like!'

'Thomas John your brother is absolutely right!'

Tee-J had the lip out and was on the dramatic side.

'I ain't got no brud no more,' he said.

'Teedge get out into the fuckin' van, would ya?'

He hadn't much choice, Tee-J, except if he was going to walk the dual carriageway, and by and by he slugged along out to the car park beside Patrick, with the polo shirt waving at them, all emotional, from the doorway. Tee-J didn't talk for a good ten minutes in the van but Mullaneys wouldn't by their nature be able to keep the silent treatment going for long.

'Fuckin' badger.'

'Tell me about it, Teedge.'

True that Patrick was near enough to fully grey at thirty-six – that ran in Mullaneys as well – and in the six months of his brother's detention it was greyer he was after getting. He wouldn't have been a bad-looking lad, he felt himself, if it wasn't for the weak chin. The chin gave him an unreliable look he was told once by a priest. Thanks very much, he said to the priest.

'What way was it inside, Teedge?'

A sullen shrug from Tee-J.

'Heard they had a head doctor at you and all?'

A raising of the eyebrows from Tee-J.

'What'd he say?'

'That I'm mad as a box of frogs. You can drop me off in Boyle.'

'Fuck off, Teedge. You money?'

'Do I look as if I have money?'

'Doggie Mannion's we've to hit so.'

'Ah fuckin' hell Patcho!'

Tee-J got a good sulk on then. Tee-J was being all seventeen as he sat there in the passenger seat of the Hitachi. Herds of fuckwads roamed the earth, was Tee-J's opinion. He reached for the dash-mounted MP3 system and he played a bit of Slayer to blank them out. Patrick drummed his fingertips on the wheel to the white-noise squall. He gave the Hitachi a nice bit of pep and Tee-J smiled despite himself. He was a kid still really. He had no patience whatsoever and after half a song's worth of Slayer, he was belting away at the search function and putting on Carcass. The MP3 system was worth more than the van, not that it was paid for.

'Gettin' the nosebleed again,' said Tee-J. 'You watchin'?'

He raised a palm to feel for the bleed and it had come sure enough. He looked at the smear on his palm and licked it. Patrick was as always disgusted by this.

'You wouldn't get it in a fuckin' kennel,' he said.

Tee-J reached for a Kleenex and wadded it and tamped it to his nostrils and he programmed the MP3 by genre, death metal on random play, and something good and fuzzy by Decimator kicked in.

'Doctor said I got wet-brain thinkin',' said Tee-J. 'Said I'd be as well staying clear of the juice.'

They listened to songs about war and leather and blood-encrusted animal pelts. Tee-J had a face on him like a kebab whatever shite he'd been eating at the unit. Patrick had read up about nutrition for adolescents in a leaflet he found in the waiting room of the clinic when he was in about the chest pains. The doctor said the chest pains were caused by stress and petrol-station coffee and signed him up to a yoga class in Rooskey. He only went the once but it was good now all the same. The woman instructor gave them all rubber yoga mats and said when things were getting bad, you found a quiet space, you closed your eyes, and you said, I'm on my mat now and that's that.

'Do we have to go to Doggie's, Patch?'

'We have to fuckin' ate, Teedge. But I know, like. I know.'

Doggie 'The Dog' Mannion lived in a holiday home scheme over the far side of the lake. A wee duplex he had bought for himself there. He was out on its patio when the boys arrived in the Hitachi. In a yellow dressing gown and a pair of swimming togs.

'Easy as we go, Patch,' said Tee-J.

There wasn't much fazed the Mullaney brothers, all told,

but a visit to Doggie did. The Dog was a large, half-bald, buttery kind of man with terrible nerves. He had the eyeliner on in thick black smudges over a deep-tan foundation like a hoor would wear. He was drinking from a child's beaker; he raised this now to salute the brothers as they crossed the communal lawn of the scheme. He put a hand inside his togs and tugged at himself briefly and the exertion caused his broad face to colour. He leaned over the patio's rail to address his visitors.

'When you get a bit of heat at all like the heat we're after getting today,' he said, 'the man below do be swimmin' in his own melt.'

A laugh was let off that sounded like a chainsaw revving. The Dog had been receiving from the Mullaneys for two years and he paid an insulting tax but he was the only operator in the vicinity who was reliable in terms of cash-flow. He led them through to the living room. Bottles of Rachmaninov vodka from Aldi were everywhere and apple-juice cartons from the same place – Apfelsaft, they called it there. Patrick lay down the box of DVDs and found that his heart was beating much too fast.

'We can't stay long, Dog,' he said.

'D'ya know I'd smoke a hunderd fags for you in a night if I was drinkin'?' said The Dog.

'DVDs for you, Dog?'

'DVDs comin' out me bollix, Mull. I no more want DVDs than the fuckin' wall.'

He eyed Tee-J.

'You're gettin' big,' he said.

He settled himself on the white plastic garden chair that was the only furniture in the place. He rubbed with the chipped black paint of his fingernails the inside of his thigh and he drank from the beaker.

'Would we say three-fifty, Doggie?'

'Don't mind your fuckin' shite-talk!'

His mood had switched instantly, as was the Mannion way, from playful to like he was going to murder you.

'Said don't mind the auld talk, Mull! Come in here and look at me like scum? Ye want my money but the way ye look at me? Like I'm a piece of fuckin' shit? All I'm to ye fellas is euro! Ye fuckin' bitches! I open my door! I offer ye the full fuckin' courtesy of my home! I . . .'

He rose and went out to his patio again. The brothers watched as he swayed out there. He looked over the waters of the lake. Patrick felt the cold dread you'd get always on a visit to The Dog but the breeze changed outside and the anger seemed to melt again: Doggie had been took by gentle thoughts.

'Forgive me,' he said, returning to the room. 'I get . . . upset in meself sometimes. I have too much love in my heart! That's the only problem with Doggie Mannion! All I want is to spend some time with ye. Would ye not take a little drink with me?'

'I'm off the juice,' said Tee-J. 'Head doctor's orders.'

'We've a rush on, Dog.'

'Ah I know,' said The Dog. ''Course my problem is I have no off-button. Are ye smellin' that by the way?'

True enough there was the queerest smell in the place. To Patrick, it was like you'd get in a welder's yard. Or maybe like a quik-dry foam-filler if you got it on your hands.

'What's it, Dog?'

Doggie winked.

155

'I'm cookin',' he said.

'Hah?'

'Ye're lookin' at the cunt,' he said, 'who's going to bring crystal methamphetamine to the County Leitrim. And ye're the boys'll help me.'

Patrick had that feeling – that the control of the night was getting away from him.

'Dog . . .'

'Hush, babies, hush,' said The Dog, and with a finger to his lips he led them towards a back room. Stronger the smell got as they came nearer to it.

Not a half-hour later the outlaw Mullaneys were headed for town in the Hitachi with two hundred euro to their name from the DVDs and seventy-seven rocks of methamphetamine, fresh-cooked, neatly packed in baggies, eleven baggies, seven rocks to the baggie. Tee-J was reading from an internet printout that Doggie had given them.

'It'll make a buck massive horny,' he said. 'A buck'll ride for twelve hours flat off a this stuff, Patch!'

Would you not, thought Patrick, get a bit cheesed off with twelve hours' worth of riding?

'Says here,' says Tee-J, 'a sure way to know a young one who's been at the meth is that she'll have fuck knots in her hair. From all the riding.'

'Fuck knots?'

'From her head slappin' up and down off the pillow, like?' said Tee-J. 'For twelve hours, Patch!'

It was great to see enthusiasm in the boy no matter what it was that put it there. The plan was they'd try offload some of the stuff in Roxy's car park when they got to town. Of course Tee-J was already burning a rock from a Diet Coke can with holes cut in.

'Arra Teedge!'

'Well I ain't drinkin',' he said. 'And don't worry, Patch. I'm definitely not gettin' into any scraps tonight.'

Of course Patrick knew sure enough what way this was ending up Tee-J-wise. There was poison and rage in the half-eejit and he hadn't licked them off the ground. There'd be the bust and the bail and the summons. And he could see himself already, stood up in the courthouse, with his white face on, explaining why the brother had failed to appear:

Tee-J gone to England, judge.

But even so the town was laid out below them as they came down the dual carriageway, and it was full of promise.

'And what are you making of it all, Mr McGurk?' said Patrick.

'Arra sure you wouldn't know which end is the toes,' said Mr McGurk.

Mr McGurk was a plastic leprechaun attached to the dashboard on a spring and he bobbed along comically as the Hitachi sped. How he had ended up being called Mr McGurk neither of them could remember. Both brothers would do Mr McGurk's voice but Tee-J did it brilliant. He did Mr McGurk as a cranky old farmer who was always giving out. Mr McGurk was six inches of green plastic but entirely alive. He was made alive by their love for each other.

'Horn on me you'd hang your coat off,' said Tee-J.

'If you were told the stuff'd make you fly you'd be feelin' for wings,' said Patrick.

Tee-J sniffed at the palm of his hand.

'That ridey-lookin' till girl still workin' at the Maxol, Patch? Girleen with the dick-stud in her tongue?'

I'm on my mat, thought Patrick Mullaney, and that's that.

There was nothing good coming. Enya's father would get a lamp on Patrick Mullaney sure as God made little apples. The guards would take badly to word about the crystal meth that was putting the hearts skaw-ways in the crowd below in Roxy's. The wire cutters was still in back of the van, he had forgotten to bring it into Doggie, and it was enough alone to put Patrick Mullaney back in Castlerea jail for a stretch. His teeth were falling out. It was greyer he was after getting. There was the situation with the lack of a roof over their heads and the situation with all the chest pains and all the stress. Tee-J's odds on staying out of scraps were long. There was only the half-chance ever of finding some peace and rest. People were fly-tipping their rubbish everywhere. Oh and the white Hitachi was set fast to its tracks and the tracks led in one direction only. The Hitachi also was making some fairly severe choking sounds. But Patrick Mullaney reckoned that if he got the exhaust sorted on her at all, she'd be 100 per cent.

DARK LIES THE ISLAND

She sat in a pool of grey-blue light thrown by the screen.
Beyond the high windows, it was darkening, the quick fade
of an October day. She had not cut in nine days but maybe
tonight. She hung a song on her cloud, Sufjan, and took
down another – she Xed a window and opened another.
There was no internet at the holiday home except for dial-
up, as though powered by a hamster on a wheel, and it
made her want to retch it was so slow. She went each day
to the cineplex at the far edge of the town. It had coin-
operated terminals in a lobby annexe upstairs. She clicked
and dragged; a deep nausea swirled. The smell of stale
popcorn and bodies rose from the main lobby beneath.
Sound FX from the movie screens, muffled, and faint
dialogue, snappy-snappy. The itch of her blood as it sped.
Gun shots. Car revs. Screams. She opened 4-Real Forum
and typed:

Maybe tonite . . .

Gretchen from Flagstaff had a green light beside her name
on the screen – Gretchen was live – and Gretchen typed:

*It is what is in your heart that must be answered it is your call
to make we are here for you, S.*

Alison from Teignmouth had a green light beside her
name on the screen – Alison was live – and Alison typed:

U hav been v strong for days why now Sara. This is what I must be asking right now. Is the med changed/weakened by ur head doc?

Kandy The Lez from Bremen had a green light beside her name – Kandy The Lez was live – and Kandy The Lez typed:

You cut tonite you photo n show me you hot fucken bitch I love you Sara K xox

The time-running-out bubble erupted on her screen – sixty seconds remaining – and she thought about it but did not insert another coin. She let the seconds come down

5, 4, 3, 2, 1

and each beat brought her deeper inside. She was upstairs in the lobby annexe. The shadows breathed. She picked up her stuff and came down the stairs three at a time and out through the lobby at blizzard pace. She crossed the car park to Apache Pizza and gorged on a four-cheese twelve-inch for its lovely seeping saturates. She was eating enough for half a rugby team and thin as a stick. Her brain was moving so fast she was losing weight. She left Apache Pizza and got in the car and gunned it for the holiday home, where she was staying, alone, on her 'year out'.

'What in Jesus' name are you going to do out there, Sara?' her father had said. 'It's going into winter, girl.'

'Just some art stuff,' she said.

Don't cut, his eyes said.

'Just give me the keys and the alarm code,' she said. 'Please?'

She had completed her Leaving Certificate in June. The

160

results came in the second week of August. She had enough points for Medicine. She had enough points for Veterinary. She had enough points to build a rocket and fly it to the moon. She hadn't slept right in months. Her skin was flawless but for the scarring on the insides of the wrists, but for the scarring on the insides of the thighs, but for the scarred remains of the smiley she had carved one night on the inside of the left ankle.

'We all have delicate complexions,' her mother had said.

We! As though a clan, or tribe, or family. The town as she pelted through had the feel of the season's quick changing, a summer killed off, a winter to come. If she floored it, she would be in time for a 1940s British stiff-upper-lip movie of the kind they showed on UK Memories channel in the early evening. Stories about war widows and valour and the last embers of hope. Ladies who had been left even more elegant and poised by the ravages of war, ladies who had been left 've-hy much ah-lone, aksherly'.

She said it aloud as she drove:

'Ve-hy much ah-lone.'

As though with marbles in her mouth:

'Ve-hy . . . mach . . . hah-lone.'

Her brain was moving so fast it was out the other side of town already and looking back. She saw herself drive. She felt like she was filmed every minute of the day. The car was a low-slung, old-school Saab in a deep wine colour. Her father was a radical architect who had reinterrogated the concept of walls. She got back to the house he had designed for family summers. It was all glass and angles and odd little nooks situated to give the eeriest, the most austere possible views across the dour bog landscape.

'Wounded', her father would call the bog, all wet-eyed as he gazed out soulfully and swirled in his hand like a gigantic glass of Masi.

The house had a bog stream run through it – there was the low constant murmuring of its brown tarry waters. She lay on the six-inch-thick glass panelling over the stream as it ran the length of the open-plan space. It wasn't a room; it was a space. Sometimes tiny eels swam through, sperm-like. Her father had driven out with her, that first weekend, and he conspicuously left every blade in the house in its place. He was phoning nightly from Granada and acting so blithe. The Sabatier kitchen knives were right there on their block. She got up and went around the room and flicked all of the lamps on.

She slid the glass doors and stepped outside and she looked back into the lit space – a magazine shot. Minus people. She turned and looked out beyond the expanse of the bog, where the ground fell away, so quickly, and there were low reefs of dune, and then a descent to superlative, untenanted coast. Each year it lost about a metre to the Atlantic – it was coming towards the house, the water. This was Clew Bay, in County Mayo, and hundreds of tiny islands were strewn down there. They were inky blobs of mood against grey water. It was a world of quiet dimly lit by the first stars and a quartermoon. The house behind her was silent as a lung.

She went back inside and crawled onto the low grey couch and sounded an animal's groan. She felt like she was sucking up all the poisons the planet had to offer. The house had been tested for radon, and there were trace elements, it was reported, and she breathed deeply, with a cupped hand in her crotch, and she tried to suck it up but radon deaths were slow. A sick tiny flutter from her crotch like the heartbeat of a gerbil. She found the remote and hit up UK Memories and sure enough there was a 1940s stiff-upper-lip playing:

'Chin up, wren, t'will soon be over!'

Vehy-mach-hah-lone. She closed her eyes for the swoon of the matinee strings. She felt the heaviness of the sorrow that hovered above – she saw it as a kind of airship. The pizza cheese re-formed and coagulated in her gut. She waited for the faces to form once more in the plate glass of the windows.

She killed the sound on UK Memories. She went around the room and flicked all of the lamps off. She went again and sat by the vague burbling of the stream. She let full dark take over the glass – that it might banish what was out there. But each night sent its visitors. The open maw of a mouth she might see or the slash of a sudden, quick turn that could only be the angle of a nose, like a Frenchman's cruel hard nose – the night put its faces to the glass. The murmuring of the stream came to work as the voices of those gathered outside.

She believed and at once did not believe.

'Please?' she whispered.

The word was enough to break the spell. She got up and went about the room and she flicked on all of the mismatched lamps – the kitsch 80s lamps, and the vintage 50s lamps, and her father's treasure, a superb thin angular 70s Belgian classic that had the look of a spider, reaching, and cost about the same as a retro Saab. Three of them made like ever. In some humourless loft in Antwerp. She slid the glass doors and stepped boldly outside and into the chill of the fresh dark.

'Nothin' and nobody,' she said.

'Veh-hy . . . much . . . hah-lone,' she said.

She convinced herself that it was so. It was chill outside but a sweet chill. The stars worked to hang a melody on the dark sky. The bogside was picked out along its expanse in an abstract confusion of shapes; the rocky outcrops and the reefed banks and the lone tree – a wind-twisted whitethorn – that was visible from the house.

'It's on holiday,' her father said once. 'Get away from all the other trees.'

The black breathing of the sea was beyond; the sea was a palpable beast, and as though it was waiting. She sniffed hard for its sexual note – brine, ozone, salt.

She turned back inside and slid the glass doors shut and every surface in the room gleamed in the lamplight with menace. The space was planed to a riot of sharp angles. The Sabatier block sat glowering on the brushed granite worktop. She shook her head rapidly from side to side, like a dog after rain. Her phone rang.

The ringtone was demented, so loud and fast, cacophonous, and she knew that it must be going on past seven o'clock – or eight o'clock, his time – in Granada. He'd have a couple of drinks down and some *jamón* and Manchego for nibbles. He'd be feeling languid and deep and thinking, okay, I'll just check in, I'll play it casual.

She had switched off voice message – it would not go to voice. So how long to let him suffer? Twenty rings? Or forty?

She answered somewhere in between.

'Hey.'

'Hey.'

The busy sound of a Spanish bar behind him, its air of

164

ease and banter, a lightness of tone, happily analytical, the spat consonants and sibilant hiss; Andalucía.

'What you been up to, Sar?'

She hated the abbreviation, its cuddle.

'Art stuff,' she said.

'You mean masturbation and smoking dope?'

A tiny smile threatened the corners of her mouth but – fuckoff! – she held firm against it.

'That sounds a little busy for me.'

A labour to his breathing gave lie to the jauntiness.

'Did you talk to your mother at all?'

'No.'

'Are you going to?'

'Please?'

'She doesn't mean to be the way she is, Sara.'

'You're defending her?'

'You know I'd be the last to. But Jesus, Sara. Just talk to her.'

A Spanish evening, behind him, and he wanted to be back there, among it – he wanted to be away.

'Go back to it,' she said.

'What?'

'Whatever it is you're doing there.'

'Sara?'

'I have a cake about done,' she said. 'A kind of meringue thing? Got to run.'

'Sara, how long is this going to go on? I mean, I know what you're going through, and I know it's been a hard, hard time.'

'You do not know.'

'I fucking know! And when it's blood, Sara, I can't just give up and not even try . . .'

'And blood has given me what exactly?'

She hung up. She turned the phone off. She went around the room and flicked all of the lamps off. She searched the dark for calm. She slid open the glass doors and stepped outside again to chill and night.

Clutch – a pair of hands took hold of her neck. She was held to the spot; a manacle grip. She felt the great restriction of breath. She tried to scream but no sound came from her mouth. It was as though in a nightmare but she was not sleeping no she was not sleeping. Hands everywhere, hands all over. Then, suddenly, a looseness, and she was freed – she dashed inside. She slid shut the glass door. She fell to the floor. She looked up to the window and the faces crowded in from all angles. The dark tunnels of their opened mouths. Then at once the faces disappeared.

She turned the phone on.

A new text message from Granada:

Give it expression.

Fuck off. She saw him thoughtfully sipping a Fino by the darkwood barrels as he texted, and thinking, I'm just so not like other dads?

The Sabatier block was a low steady throbbing in the dark of the open space. She cut for the red vibrancy, for feeling. See the royal red army march in jagged lines down the pale hillside.

She went around the room and turned all of the lamps on. She searched for the laptop. The dial-up was so slow she had to put the laptop out of her sight so as not to burst into flames of fury.

Her father had said:

'You're not mad, Sara. You're just addicted to the fucking internet.'

Which did not explain the clutching at her throat or the gleam of menace from cut-steel door handles or the faces at the windows or the medication; it did not explain all of the medication.

Her mother had new tits since Christmas.

She pushed back the couch and she found the laptop underneath and she brought it to the cable by the retro phone desk – a fucking cable! – and she plugged it and hit connect:

Gremlin voices gurgled from the medieval depths of dial-up.

Every inch of her skin burned with itch. She went to find some music. She had forgotten to bring the iPod dock to the house and there was only the 'sound system', as he called it, which made her smile, and there were only CDs.

Discs!

She flicked through:

Synchronicity by The Police.

Jesus.

Astral Weeks by Van Morrison.

Who looked like an especially sweaty oompah-loompah.

Revolver by The Beatles.

She played 'For No One' back-to-back eight times. She would not play it again because she had feelings about the dark significance of the number nine. She knew she should prefer the John tracks, but. She knew that John bought an island in Clew Bay, in the 1960s, but there were three hundred and sixty-five islands down there, and she could not say which one. Dorinish Island – her father claimed to know it, by sight, he said you could see it from a high vantage beside the house. John sailed a psychedelic caravan across the bay

167

on a raft once but he never ended up living on Dorinish, with Yoko, as planned.

She went to dial-up.

The forum took eleven minutes to load.

She headbutted the couch.

'Dorinish' – the word lolled on her tongue, and repeated; it sounded like an artisanal cheese or a seaweed therapy facility.

There was just one green light on 4-Real forum for live – Gretchen from Flagstaff.

Sara typed:

I think I'm going to do it tonite?

And the green of the light for live on Gretchen at once died.

She ripped the cable from the laptop. She slid open the glass doors. She flung the laptop out into the dark. It must have landed somewhere but it did so without a sound. As though it had been caught?

She went to the bathroom and split open her pills to wash the powders away, the pinks and greens, the mica-gleam of the powders, and then the dull mulch as they clotted in the tapwater, and the clots swirled a moment, and disappeared. She opened her mouth and looked inside and saw the healthful pink of her gums and the arch of her jawbone.

The sound of a text message drew her back to the *space* and the stream murmured, ominously; the message was from her mother:

Weather here great, how weather there? Any goss? Art going well?

Her mother was in the Tarn Valley, in France. She had married a former broker from Dublin who had bought a failing vineyard there. Her mother's voice she could no longer bear to hear – it was high and trilling, it was from the valley of the squeaks. Texts were by now the limit of their interaction; this was understood. Her mother had cheekbones, new tits, an indulgent smile.

Sara texted:

Weather here glorious! Busy busy. Love lots! S xxx.

It was better to enter the contract of vapidity than to try to reason out the madness of that smile, or try to see past the cheekbones, the perfect teeth, the rampant-teenage-bunny tits.

Not to mention the little pink dresses.

Next came a shrapnel attack on the plate glass surrounds – a sudden assault of rain from the bay. She went around the room and turned off all the lamps. Her mind was moving so quick she felt the rain in her face before she slid open the doors and stepped outside.

A cloud mass travelled low over the bay, and now the quartermoon was obscured, and the rain came hard and slantwise, and there was a wind up to give an eeriness and she beamed ecstatically as the rain came through. It was generous and capable and soaked her to the bone in seconds flat.

She went back inside and stepped out of her clothes and shivered and she thought that maybe tonight she would cut on the inside of her thigh, top left, just there. The Sabatier block brooded in night's shadow like a waiting bishop. She was moved to approach it.

Because this is not going to improve, Sara. This is blood-deep and malevolent. This is for always.

Thus the Dark Angel did whisper; thus did its soft words creep.

As she crossed the floor, she stumbled on the TV remote, and hit the mute on/off: the sound boomed again on UK Memories. It was advertising a new box set of Beatles remasters. It was playing 'For No One'. The ninth time of listening, and she stood frozen in her step until the song had finished – a Message, unquestionably. But she picked up the remote and killed the TV.

And then the rain eased and played a slower beat on the plate glass in brush strokes. She went around the room and flicked all the lamps on. She went to the Sabatier block. She carefully withdrew the nine knives of the set. She carried two in one hand, three in the other and two wedged under each arm. She went towards the dark. She bent and slid open the plate glass doors with her mouth.

Outside.

She let the knives fall by her feet. The night about was breathing, unwebbed, darkscreened. She picked the first knife up, a serrated-edge breadknife, and she swung a few practice turns of an overarm arching movement, and then she threw the knife far out into the night. The way the ball of her arm twisted so efficiently in the shoulder socket – the satisfaction of that. She threw all of the knives – one by one – and each was taken by the dark and she could not see but could feel the way each was taken noiselessly by the boggy ground.

She went back inside and wrapped herself in the first thing she could find – his hipster duffelcoat, in a retro mustard shade, from the rack; waft of fathermusk.

And she stepped outside again, to be among it, and she walked in bare feet to the high vantage. She looked down on the dark of Clew Bay and the tiny islands that lay in the murk. The cloudbank shifted, a fraction, as though cued by a smiling choreographer, and light fell from the quarter-moon and picked out a single island – a low, oblong shape – and it was lit for a moment's slow reveal. She took a step that was a step outside, yet again, as though from a chrysalis, or trap. Darkly below the moving sheets of water were reliable, never-changing, mesmeric. The hill shapes picked out against the night; the islands, and the Atlantic beyond. She sat on the wet ground. She closed her eyes and knitted her hands around her knees. She huddled closer to herself, and went deeper. She closed her eyes and allowed the world without to fade, for a small while anyway, and for a half a minute, and then a whole one – and then more – there was something just a little like sleep.

BERLIN ARKONAPLATZ – MY LESBIAN SUMMER

i

Silvija turned to me from the studio couch and said:

'Patrick, I am going to teach you everything you need to know about the female genitalia.'

I was at this moment twenty-one years old and coming to terms with the cold hard fact of my genius.

'But I've got a terrible trembling sensation in my hands,' I said. 'I'm not sure now is the ideal time for genitals.'

'Patrick,' she said. 'You are not going to be using your hands.'

She sat on the couch, in her underwear, with a scarred Macbook perched on her strong, thin, walnut-cracker thighs. She smoked as only a Slav can smoke – *devouring* her smoke. She had a flicky fringe and superstar cheekbones. Technically, she was lesbian, but there appeared to be movement on the matter.

'Patrick,' she said. 'Take your clothes off and get out of bed.'

Even in early summer, the studio was cold as the steppe, and I would put extra layers on to sleep. Silvija was born in the teeth of the wind of an actual steppe and she did not feel the cold. She put aside the laptop, and she stood and eyed me derisively as I approached. With a thumb and forefinger she massaged a nipple. She had small tits but enormous nipples.

'If you do okay, I will kiss you,' she said. 'But only once.'

She turned out to be as good as her word on this, and the kiss was not the least of her gifts to me.

ii

By her own reckoning, Silvija was at this time the most brilliant fashion photographer in all of Berlin. This didn't mean that she got paid. The magazines she worked for tended to fold after an issue or two. And *Vogue* wasn't going to come calling anytime soon. Asked to photograph, say, a vampy spike-heeled ankle boot, Silvija would commit to print only the leather of its sole, and that blurrily, as some meth-thinned model, wearing latex knickers and a sneer, aimed a high kick at the camera, down some malevolent alleyway with gemstones of broken glass – Berlin diamonds – scattered to sparkle all around.

'But you don't really see the boot, Silvija?'

'I do not photograph the motherfucking boot, Patrick. I photograph the motherfucking life!'

Money was always tight, and we supplemented the magazine work by shoplifting, breaking and entering, and hiring out to the younger designers as they compiled their portfolios. The designers were routinely troublesome – I remember the schizophrenic Croat with his pioneering cutting technique, the polyamorous Frenchman who weighed about as much as a bag of feathers and was reinventing the frock coat, and the epileptic Tasmanian allegedly wanted in Australia for setting fire to a model during Melbourne Fashion Week.

We descended the eerie stairwell from the studio. We emerged onto Arkonaplatz in the morning. The nicotine burn of her kiss was on my lips still. The sun had come strongly through; already the tables were full outside the cafés. We stopped for tiny smoking thimbles of black coffee at Niko's, and I felt some prose coming on. Silvija shook her head in amusement at my lovelorn state.

'There will be no honeymoon, Patrick,' she said. 'You did fine. And there will be further business between us. There will be instruction. But do you know how much it means to me?'

She snapped her fingers to indicate the sheer nothingness of what had that morning occurred, and I nodded glumly in understanding.

'Got it?'

'Yes.'

Silvija snapped her fingers like this a lot. She allowed weight to nothing. All of life, she implied, was without meaning or lasting import, and in this way, I believe, she was teaching me how I should operate (and how I should think) if I truly intended to be an artist. We left the muddy remains of our coffees, stubbed our Marlboro Lights, and set out for a towerblock in the district of Wedding, there to photograph for the deranged Tasmanian model-burner a double-jointed Turkish neurotic capering with a string of anal beads.

And a Rottweiler.

The Berlin designers had until this time mostly lived and worked in Prenzlauer Berg. By 2005, however, the bohemian bourgeoisie from five continents were arriving for the quarter's cut-price lofts and superb childcare facilities, and gentrification was fast spreading through the old tenements and squares.

'Motherfucking breeders,' Silvija called the new arrivals.

The fashion crowd generally was in arch dismay at the intrusion, and had started to venture north from P'berg into the riskier neighbourhoods of Wedding. This was where most of the serious shoots happened that summer. We stopped at a corner shop on the way for some bottles of pils. I uncapped mine with the opener chained to the counter, Silvija hers with her teeth. We drank pils more or less constantly and ate very rarely. We crossed Bremenstrasse, dodging the ironically bearded cyclists on their high-nellies, and breathed in the petrol views. I lugged all the gear; Silvija *strode*. Inclined as always to be artistically late, we lay for a while on the scraggy hilltop in Mauerpark. We slipped in an earpiece each from my headphones and listened religiously to the Nina Simone version of 'Lilac Wine'. We looked out across the city.

'I give it six months,' Silvija said, and spat dramatically.

I was only a few months off the plane from Cork but Silvija had ten years of Berlin under her belt, and she allowed me to share the old-hand snootiness that those years granted; I had learned to affect the same languid woe as all the other old hands. A constant of hip cities is that much of the conversation centres around the fact the city is not as hip as once it was. In Mauerpark that morning, Silvija talked seriously for the first time of leaving Berlin behind, and I felt a terrible spike of nausea.

'Don't worry,' she said. 'Not for a while yet.'

We flung our empty bottles and made for the shoot. She hoicked another of her awful thick green phlegmy spits and I tried not to notice. She was so lean, with a ferocious mouth, and XXX-rated eyelashes. I'd found her through a small ad – a share offered on a studio apartment. The sense memory of the morning's events was still with me. First the mouth, and after a long time my hands had stopped trembling enough to be brought into play. She talked me through the operation. It was delicate stuff. My hands felt so heavy, but then she laid hers on mine to guide, and lifted the weight – everything was suddenly lighter.

iv

Wedding was a raw expanse of towerblocks, tattoo pits, kebab shops. Nogoodniks in mauve-coloured tracksuits decorated every corner. We had a properly respectful air as we passed through. This was how Berlin was supposed to be. We cut down a back way, for a while, to avoid the main drag, because the sight of the kebab gyros was sickening Silvija's stomach, which was troublesome. The rearsides of the towerblocks loomed either side of a dirt pathway itchy with catkins beneath our sandals, and the word 'proletariat' rolled its glamorous syllables over my tongue. Silvija may have been lazy as a feline in her stride but she made as sly and sure-footed a progress. She wore black military fatigues cut off at the knee and a black vest a couple of sizes too small the better to ride sexily high on her waist. Just as we approached the tenement where the shoot would take place, Silvija received a call to say the Tasmanian had 'technically died' that morning but the show would go on.

There were always such complications. The Tasmanian's assistant, a serene Vietnamese, was instead in charge when we reached the old apartment where the shoot would happen. Politely, we asked after the designer.

'At six a.m.?' the Vietnamese grinned. 'Clinical death! Now? Much improve!'

The room was peopled with hipster flunkies, and the Turkish model was in place. She had a pair of recent stab wounds in her side and looked as if she had walked straight off a human rights-type poster about torture. Silvija began to set up – she would not go digital and used commie-era Leicas always. I attempted to calm the model who was mouthing vengeance of death against a two-timing girl-friend. The anal beads and the Rottweiler were introduced. Silvija declared that the dog lacked a sufficiently vicious mien and she smashed a camera lens off the wall. She attempted to goad the dog to promote a viciousness but there was no response, and the shoot, as so often, broke down into a period of tense analysis. Pils was sent for to help smooth the debate. It went not well, even so, with Silvija questioning the talents of the absent Tasmanian.

'Motherfucker calls himself a designer,' she said. 'And his autumn fucking accessory? Anal fucking beads! Once again with the anal fucking beads!'

In my innocence, I did not know the exact purpose of anal beads, and I confided as much to the Turkish model.

'Is sex toy,' she said. 'Lots and lots of glitter beads on a chain. These beads they get bigger in sequence. What you do with these beads . . .'

I put a hand to my empty stomach, and pleaded.

Silvija opened the scarred laptop and mailed the Tasmanian – he was apparently online even in intensive care – and sprayed some heavy snark about his autumn accessories. The Vietnamese clucked contentedly and went to the kitchen zone and stirfried some scallions and chicken gizzards. The flunkies lounged in hipster bliss, and then fizzed madly and loudly for a few moments – looking for knickers or garter belts – and then lounged some more. The Turkish model stroked the inside of my arm and said she was not exclusively homo and had always liked redheads. I was on a roll with ladies who liked ladies. Eventually some photos were taken. The Rottweiler took a dump in the middle of the floor. Silvija said:

'Perfect! We use the shit!'

This was the Berlin fashion scene, in the summer of 2005, in the district of Wedding. There was a lot of heroin and a lot of dog shit. Everybody was thin and gorgeous.

And Jesus, did we smoke.

v

I was finding out how carelessly life might be lived. The people I met through Silvija were all addictions and stylish madness. Every other hour, there was a crack-up, or an arrest, or an abortion, or somebody jumped out a window, or fucked an Austrian heiress, and every deranged turn of events was so gladly met and swirled with. They were attuned to the wild moment, while I was yet nervous, careful, locked to the past. It seemed to me that they had all grown up godless and without foul repressions. They had not grown up sitting on three-piece suites of floral design in the beige suburbs. They had not come to adult-hood in rooms laid with unpleasantly diamond-patterned carpets bought off the travellers at the markets of drab Irish towns. How can I begin to explain? Does it suffice to say that the olive oil in my childhood home was kept in the bathroom? It was bought at the chemist shop and drizzled mournfully onto my father's problem scalp. Hair was never good for our people, generally, perhaps on account of the remorseless wind that assaults the sides of west Limerick mountains. It is no exaggeration to say that the male fore-bears of my clan – my father and his brothers – were scarred by wind. They all had the permanently startled look that comes from working outside in hard gusts, and something of it had been passed onto me, this look; even though I had never myself stood in the teeth of a force six gale wrestling a stuck cow from the boggy sump of a ditch; even though I spent my time writing lurid short stories and (increasingly perceptive and subtle) essays about the emergence of Italian Neo-Realism in the 40s, and the troubled legacy of the Nouvelle Vague.

Silvija, of course, was fanatically well read. She read every-thing and in six languages. She had informed me quietly that I was a genius. She told me that I was the culmination of Irish literature. (She said it 'litra-chure'.) It had all been leading up to me.

She had such faith.

The shoot broke down into the usual chaos. There were taunts and ultimatums. Silvija and I walked. We decided to go instead and rob some Americans. There was a roost of them in our building. They were on the floor directly beneath the studio. We could hear the insect trilling of their talk down there.

'When the Americans appear,' Silvija said, 'it means that Berlin is officially over. May it rest in peace. Amen.'

Daily, the gauche and Conversed hordes priced out of San Francisco and Brooklyn were arriving, with their positivity, their excellent teeth and their MFAs. They could be spotted a mile off in the clubs – their clothes were wrong, their hair was appalling and their dancing was just terrible.

We rang the bell on their apartment. We listened. It was empty – they must have been out photographing the TV tower or taking rides in the tourist-rental Trabants. We went upstairs to our studio and shinned down from the studio balcony to theirs. We quickly made through the place. We found eight hundred dollars in the drawer of a vanity and two passports – Becky Cobb and Corey Mutz, in chunky retro eyewear both – and we took these also. There was a price to be had for American passports from the Ukrainians who drank at Dieter's. We left the way we had come – Silvija climbed like a jungle cat; I laboured. But we made it, and we went and had us a royal day on the town.

In a vast Old German-type trough, we stuffed ourselves with many potato based dishes and many enormous sausages. We drank exquisite Burgundy and Bavarian whisky. And pils. We touched each other beneath the tablecloth. What Silvija could do with her toes was extraordinary. She taught me, phonetically, the choruses of some enchanting childhood songs of the steppe.

'But what are these songs about?' I asked.

'Mostly they are about oxen and death,' she said.

We left the restaurant and went to Dieter's. It was a low bar on Schönhauser Allee, and there we had more pils and a rendezvous with the scarred and mysterious Hoods of Kiev. These were among the characters lately populating my stories but I could get them only palely. There was no way to render with a still-callow pen the force of intrigue stored in the black heat of Victor's eyes, nor the sexual languidity in the way that Xcess (as she styled herself) drained her glass, nor the . . . I just couldn't get it down right. We made another two hundred euro from the passports. We left the bar and walked down the street – the plan was to buy some new and impractical shoes. There was the rumble above us of the elevated trains. I complained at the lack of true lustre in my stories. Silvija sighed and stopped up on the pavement and she took hold of my elbow. She gave me one of her statements or manifestos, then, one of her great orations on the Nature of Art:

'When you are worried, that is when you are working. When you are doing nothing, that is when the work is happening. It does not happen in the front section of the brain, Patrick. It happens in back section. Here is the subconscious level. This is the place the story come from. You just have to let it happen. Liberate yourself! If it is going to come, it will come. You just make yourself available and open to it. If it comes good, some day, it comes good. Champagne! But you have no power over it. It is all involving luck. When it feels like nothing is happening, that is when it is all happening. And remember that when you are worried, you are working.'

Still I search for a more succinct explanation of how it all occurs, but I know I will not find one.

vii

It was in odd scraps and rags that Silvija's own story came through to me. Mostly in the small hours, when deep in her cups and whuzzled from the hashpipe, when in that borderland between wakefulness and sleeping, with her eyes half closed, wrapped in blankets against the night chill, this is when she would tell me of the viking-level horrors she had witnessed and been a part of: the rape, the pillage, the evil marauding. War-lands I could not imagine. And Silvija as a scared child among it all – Silvija scared was even harder to imagine. Such a story I had in my selfish way yearned for – maybe I could steal it, and recast it, and it would lend my work the gravitas it lacked; writers are such *maggots,* especially the young ones – but as she fed it to me in these night-time crumbs, I could not even begin to process the detail. I have made myself forget most of it. I know that she had as a kid dispensed blow jobs for soup money. She had been tied up in a facility once and brutalised with a broom handle. She had escaped but only to long broken years trailing madly through the squats of Barcelona (held captive once by a Sudanese in El Born, she had been made to eat catfood) and then there was a period of home-lessness in Genoa (she cracked up and became obsessed with reading the words of the streetname signs backwards – Via Garibaldi . . . Idlabirag) and it was Berlin before she recovered, it was Berlin where she found her talents and the balance of her humours and the makings of a hard shell.

Nights at the studio she would go to the bathroom and spit blood in the sink. She would wash it away but I would find on the porcelain smeared traces in the mornings.

viii

The summer deepened, and our days became toned with sadness, and other, unnameable things. I sat up in bed one morning, smoking. I tapped the ash into an empty pils bottle. Silvija squatted on her heels on the couch, in her underwear, battering the laptop – she had a wide circle of acquaintance, 80 per cent of which she was feuding with at any given time. The light poured in from the climbing sun, and caught her bare, brown muscles. The windfall from the Americans and the passports was long since consumed and we were again in the depths of poverty, but we looked pretty good poor. The Wedding scene was slow, due to the season and the usual inclemence of luck that afflicted the fashion people: the arrests, the random plagues, the near-death experiences. This particular morning, there was something like shyness between us. Briefly, in the night, Silvija's strict no-penetration dictat had been lifted. I knew even at the moment it was a mistake, despite the luxuriousness of the sensation. I could feel the scaredness in her. I knew that it would never happen again. And I knew in my heart that I just wasn't working out as a lesbian. I was too clumsy and knuckly.

Not that she didn't walk with me the hot summer streets of noon, and not that she didn't teach me, and not that she didn't give me something, just a tiny sustaining something, of her great aura.

I believe it was that same day, in the beer garden on Kastanienallee, that she turned the camera on me, there beneath the chestnut trees in full leaf, and I was shy of the lens and awkward but she told me what to do.

'You don't look at it,' she said. 'You look through it.'

I have the photograph still and it is sacred to me. On the wooden bench between us, in the amber of a stein glass, she is reflected, with her camera raised. She is there, blurrily, and it's just a shade, but it is all that I have left of her.

ix

The end came sharply. I woke one morning to find Silvija packing her stuff. That holdall of hers had seen plenty. I tried to sound casual but there was boy-fear in my tone.

'So this is it?' I croaked.

'You knew it was coming,' she said.

The studio had had its time, she said. She was going to stay with a girlfriend in Kreuzberg. It was time that I stood on my own two feet.

'You need to go find your own life, Patrick,' she said.

'Yeah and you need to go to a fucking doctor!'

I was so angry to be cast aside and I was lost in the city without her. I became depressed. I stayed with some other people for a while, in Mitte – artists, of course – but they all by contrast with Silvija seemed to be acting parts, and I have forgotten all their names. I knew that the sweet days of the summer had passed and it was time to fly away. Reluctantly, she came to the station on the morning I was to leave for the airport. She hugged me on the platform but so awkwardly; she fled instantly from the hug. She said she would email and that I could phone but six years have passed and never once did she reply to an email, never once did she answer her phone, and after a few months, the line was dead.

Which signifies nothing, necessarily, because Silvija changed phones all the time. And anyway I must believe that she is out there, somewhere among the dreaming cities of Europe, maybe in Trieste, or in Zagreb, or in Belgrade again. I must believe that she is out there, still beautiful, foul-mouthed and inviolate.

KEVIN BARRY won the Rooney Prize for Irish Literature for *There Are Little Kingdoms,* his debut collection of stories. His novel, *City of Bohane,* won the International IMPAC Dublin Literary Award, the European Union Prize for Literature, and the Authors' Club First Novel Award and was shortlisted for the Hughes & Hughes Irish Novel of the Year Award and the Costa First Novel Award. *Dark Lies the Island* was shortlisted for the Frank O'Connor International Short Story Award and includes stories published in the *New Yorker* and *Best European Fiction* as well as the winning story of the 2012 Sunday Times EFG Private Bank Short Story Award. Barry also works as a screenwriter and a playwright. He lives in County Sligo, Ireland.

Typeset in Dante MT by Palimpsest Book Production Ltd.
Manufactured by Versa Press on acid-free,
30 percent postconsumer wastepaper.